Lois rubbed m
as we lay in the dar

"We're genetically geared to compete, but also to cooperate," she said as if in a review session. "For survival of the species. Remember that time we rode the jeepney together going to Midsayap? Where I tried to ride the bumper with you?"

"They wouldn't let you," I reminisced with her. "You're a woman. Women tire more easily, but also, women fall off more easily. Or if there's an accident or ambush, no one wants to see a woman suffer."

"Exactly," Lois said. "Survival of the fittest includes gallantry of the strong to protect the weak. Remember what that man said to me to get me to go inside? He tapped me on the shoulder. That's what they do. They tap on the shoulder and say, *I will be the one*. I will be the one to take the hardship and danger. That is so beautiful, so touching."

She turned fully on her side as if to look at me, even though we were in total darkness.

"When we get married someday, Mississippi, that's going to be our wedding vow. Before you kiss the bride to seal our marriage, we're going to face each other, look each other in the eyes, hold both hands, and say to each other—"

She placed her hand on my cheek for emphasis. "Let's say it now. I want to vow it right now. Let's do it."

"I will be the one," we said to one another.

"Whenever one of us is weak," she continued, "the other will be there. We will always be there for each other. We will always survive."

We sealed our vow with a kiss.

I Will Be the One

by

Larry Farmer

I Will Be the One

Cover Art by *Tina Lynn Stout*

The Wild Rose Press, Inc.
PO Box 708
Adams Basin, NY 14410-0708
Visit us at www.thewildrosepress.com

Publishing History
First Vintage Rose Edition, 2015
Print ISBN 978-1-62830-703-0
Digital ISBN 978-1-62830-704-7

Dedication

To Luke, Lesley, and Monette and her beautiful family.
And in loving memory and gratitude to Larry Foley.

Chapter 1

So many thoughts race through my mind while watching the news of the pro-Russian demonstrations and riots in the Ukraine, the downing of aircraft, both military and civilian, by pro-Russian rebels inside the country, accompanied by the massing of Russian troops on their border. Russia's invasion of the Crimea was but a few months before. Now some fear another Cold War, even World War III perhaps, as Russia's defiant leader thumbs his nose at the West. And there is always concern over possible disruption of the already teetering world economy.

I scan the channels further and see reports of turmoil in the Middle East. What is happening? Fear grips me. A feeling of vulnerability. Will there be anything left of the world I've known? How will this affect our lives in America? Nothing feels far away in this age of globalization, especially knowing friends I've made abroad face this more directly.

So many thoughts. But in my case, so many memories. As a baby boomer, I lived most of my life during the Cold War era. There were bases overseas to protect. Dictators to thwart or prop up. Military alignments to enhance. The more things change the more they stay the same, the saying goes.

I was a Marine during the Vietnam conflict. Although I wasn't sent, I volunteered to go. Not just to serve my country. I took the threat of a Communist menace seriously. With Communism came massive executions, concentration camps, and bullying. Endless intrigue and power politics. I wanted to do something. To make a difference. I was such an idealist. I wanted so badly to serve.

After that war I was restless. Stuck in a materialistic aftermath. Trapped and snug in the naïveté of prosperity and security, I felt like a cog of conformity wallowing in the mundane. With advanced skills in wealth creation from my master's degree in economics at Ole Miss, I was bored and frustrated, to be blunt. I wanted something in my life. And I still wanted to make a difference. To serve in some capacity. To give of myself.

They called it the toughest job you'll ever love. My papers were being processed for the United States Peace Corps, in late summer of 1983, when I saw on the news there was an assassination. In a country called the Philippines, a political reformist by the name of Benigno Aquino was gunned down on the tarmac of the Manila International Airport. Little did I know then how, because of that event, my fate and my experiences in the Peace Corps would intertwine and change my life forever.

At six feet and a hundred ninety pounds, I still had my Marine physique and muscle tone. Though it was the Peace Corps I was joining now, things didn't sound so peaceful to me. I was glad I was big. Though in a non-combatant's role, I wasn't so sure I wouldn't have to be on my guard. With no combat gear at my disposal, I could physically thwart the more marginal threats that might come my way, and most importantly, the Marines had conditioned my psyche. I knew what to do with danger.

There was a song that followed me around in those Peace Corps days after I arrived at my assigned destination. "Ang Bayan Ko" it was called. In English you would simply say "My Country." I heard these words sung only in Tagalog, but the English translation is moving. I could tell you of the meaning they held for me, but it would be cheating the Filipinos, for this song is theirs. The story, however, about my days with them during this time, is hopefully for everyone.

This love song was originally written as a poem by Jose Corazon de Jesus:

> The country mine, the Philippines,
>> land of gold and flowers.
> Love is in its destiny,
>> offered beauty and splendor.
> And, for its refinement and beauty,
>> foreigners were enticed.
> Country mine, enslaved wert thou,
>> mired in suffering.
> Even birds that are free to fly—
>> cage you them and they shall cry!
> What more a nation, most verily beautiful,
>> would not yearn to break free?
> Philippines of mine that I treasure,
>> cradle of my tears and suffering,
>> my ambition
>> is to see thee truly free!

Chapter 2

"A package arrived for you, James," my mother said in her soft Southern drawl as she handed it to me. "Is this what you've been waiting for?"

I tore it open and nodded that it was. "It's from the Peace Corps," I explained. "They just assigned me to the Philippines. Maybe here's some third-world version of Hawaii, I'm hoping."

I read the brochures and pamphlets in front of her as she cooked, occasionally reading aloud.

"Over seven thousand islands," I nearly swooned, looking up as I pictured it. Mother smiled as if living the dream with me. "They speak English, and most are Catholic," I continued.

"For once you'll seem a mainstream American," she replied. "You won't stick out so much because you're Jewish."

I got out some of my mother's Hawaiian record albums, which was as close as I could get to Filipino culture, I assumed. "Tiny Bubbles." I drove everyone crazy playing that song constantly on the stereo and humming it everywhere I went. I also bought a video of *The King And I*, though that was about Siam.

It was obvious by how little my parents talked about it that they were embarrassed I was going into the Peace Corps. That's because where we're from, Vicksburg, Mississippi, people think Yankees and

4

liberals do this stuff. And all that money to get a master's in economics at Ole Miss—just for this?

It must be the Jewish thing about us, people decided, when they heard what I was about to do. The John F. Kennedy vision and such, you know. They were certain that by now President Reagan should have already disbanded the Peace Corps.

Chapter 3

When I arrived at the Manila International Airport in February 1984 in a group of prospective Peace Corps Volunteers and looked out the window at the miles of ghetto around me, it took every ounce of idealism I had to stay.

But other things were brewing that overshadowed that view.

The airport was under military control, cordoned off. Some fifty thousand demonstrators stood outside, protesting the murder of Benigno "Ninoy" Aquino. Murdered, in fact, right at this airport six months before.

"Please don't worry," a representative of the Peace Corps told us at customs. "I have a diplomatic clearance to get all new Peace Corps personnel out of the airport despite the military lockdown," she assured us.

To the right of the airport was a chain-link fence surrounding the lower open perimeter of the building. The fence was covered with hundreds of protestors, silently waiting. At the top of the fence was a small open space, just big enough for protestors to crawl over after climbing the fence. On the left, adjacent to us, were a hundred or so riot police, fully encased in protective riot gear, large shields in front of each man, and each wielding a long wooden club. An eerie silence surrounded us. I could hear only heavy breathing as each side waited for the other to make a move.

We left them behind as a Peace Corps bus took us to a section of Manila called Malate, which was near a beach where the hotels were for tourists, a huge step up from my first impression. I was even a tad disappointed, actually. I had come to live among the downtrodden. It bothered my conscience to so quickly experience much comfort.

I already had a best friend in our group. A girl I'd met back at the staging area for Peace Corps prospects in San Diego. A graduate of Ohio State named Lois. We sat together on the plane to Manila and got quite chummy, even sharing shoulders to take naps along the way. She was cute, with long, frizzy, light-brown hair, and had a nice figure. It made being friends appealing since we probably were going to be stuck out in the middle of nowhere after we finished training. It was good to know someone would be out there with me, or near me, wherever "out there" was. A place I could run away to during free periods. R-and-R we'd called such times in the Marines. Meaning rest and relaxation. A smart, robust, good-looking girl with some sass filled the order perfectly for me.

There were dorm-like areas for us to stay in while being processed in Manila. They were clean and tidy, but the Peace Corps was already limiting how much they were going to spend on us, not wanting to spoil us before dumping us into the squalor where we'd probably soon be living.

Right off, my cohorts dubbed me the Mississippi Redneck, which shortened to Mississippi, which soon became my name to them instead of James. After I got assigned to the Central Bank of the Philippines, some of these same associates viewed me with contempt, as if I wanted to foreclose people's farms.

I don't know if it derived from being one of the few Jews in Vicksburg, Mississippi—one of the few Jews in or around anything about Mississippi, for that matter—but I never enjoyed just hanging around with whomever. I need companionship and interaction, but I don't enjoy small talk, or trying to fit in. I never was a loner, but I preferred spending most of my time by myself.

Lois, however, was a different story in my eyes. I don't know why we hit it off so well, but we did, and it was instantaneous, almost with the first hello in San Diego. She sought me out, to be blunt. *Who was this guy from Mississippi?* Those were almost her exact words. That and openly wondering why I didn't have a hooked nose, you know, like Jews are supposed to have. Or why I stood six foot tall, which didn't fit the bill in her eyes, since Jews were supposed to be short. She was at least satisfied I had brown eyes and brown wavy hair like I was supposed to have. But her questions seemed more curiosity than anything hostile or skeptical. Maybe she wasn't as blunt about it as I'm portraying, but I determined she was subtle only to keep from being perceived as someone who stereotypes. Stereotyping was supposed to be my department, since I was from Mississippi.

She never thought she would meet anyone from such a place as Mississippi, and surely not with the same agenda as serving in a culturally sensitive organization like the United States Peace Corps. The fact that I was Jewish answered some of that for her, but it still seemed an oxymoron to her that the same mindset could inhabit both a demography of Peace Corps and the heart of Dixie.

Lois and I paired off on our first afternoon in Manila, while determining our skills and desires in how to best serve the Peace Corps mission. If we separated for an interview with someone, or for shots, or with a distinct discussion group, we immediately sought each other out afterwards to compare the experience and information.

When released for the day to discover what we chose of Malate, we checked out the sights together. As in: together we two, apart from the others in the group.

It was hot and muggy on the streets of Malate, even at night. It reminded me of Mississippi in the summer. Manila Bay, part of the Pacific Ocean between the Philippines and the South China Sea, was barely a block away, but the buildings and the density of the compressed human population all but offset any moderating breeze there might have been.

"Which way you want to go?" I asked her, in case she had any ideas of what she wanted to do for the evening.

"There's a folk house nearby," Lois said as we walked out into the street from the hotel. "I heard one of our directors talk about it in a cultural lecture this afternoon. He made a big deal about it. He said to be sure to go tonight, in particular, because the Filipino Bob Dylan sings tonight. It's called the Hobbit House. The waiters there are all dwarves."

"Okay." I began to read the signs of the establishments on the street we walked. "Hobbit House." I hummed. "I'm looking for the Hobbit House." I looked at her for clarification. "Which direction?"

"I was told turn right after we left our hotel. Turn right and look across the street to the left as we walk. It's a couple or so blocks from the hotel."

"There," I said, pointing. "Fifty yards or so on the left, just like you heard."

Lois winked at me in celebration, then grabbed my hand and held it as we walked. The problem with that was I loved it. The problem with loving it was I didn't want to. I knew how this Mother Nature thing works with our DNA and our hormones and all. One of the appeals so far about Lois was it was so easy to be friends.

Friends.

That's all I wanted. Not even a good time at her expense. Just friends. Safety type friendship. We were going to be a couple of hours from each other when we finished training, so it was explained to us by the Filipino Area Project Coordinator we had together. Meaning we would see each other now and then, mind our own business, do our jobs, save the world, and go back home. Or in my case, hopefully, to Hawaii.

But here I was, holding her hand as we walked to the Hobbit House to hear the Filipino Bob Dylan. *Please,* I begged myself as we walked along, *be careful while you have the chance. Please don't get carried away now, then spend empty nights in a hot, dirty room in the middle of nowhere, in the Philippines, thinking of a girl you can't have.*

As we crossed the street to enter the Hobbit House, I acknowledged to Lois how the place had appeal. As good a place as any to know something of our new setting.

The Hobbit House had many American patrons. *Somehow this was the place to be*, I decided. It must be chic or something. Cool. It did have atmosphere. Like a place you would expect in the Greenwich Village area of New York. Or so I visualized. Where the real folk-singing Bob Dylan got his start.

The singer on stage, Freddie Aguilar, was tall for a Filipino, and dark skinned, even more so than most. He had long, black, stringy hair that flowed under a cowboy-type hat. I asked one of the Americans at the table next to us if this guy indeed was who we came to see. The so-called Filipino Bob Dylan. The man I asked verified it was so.

While looking at the menu, made up mostly of American food items, I liked hearing the singer already. His voice was resonant, and he had his performance down. I had to assume it was a performance, that he must do it so much it was routine, but it seemed as sincere as anything I ever saw from a stage.

"We'll be learning Tagalog," Lois said in conversation while we waited for our food. "When we get to training. Did you catch that? That's the main dialect, you know. But after all the colonizing, Tagalog is about a third Spanish words now. Some say Taglish, anymore, made up of English words thrown in, too. Did your instructor mention how there were eighty-seven dialects in the Philippines? But Tagalog is the national dialect, the one spoken here on the big island, Luzon, and in particular, in Manila."

"Why will we learn the national one, if we're going to be trained in Mindanao and live there afterwards?"

"Perhaps to not offend other groups speaking other dialects. Mindanao is more recently settled. It's really more like colonized by other Filipino groups. So many groups from other islands have settled there in a hodgepodge in the last century or two. Even now as the Philippine population keeps growing, I was told, there's a lot of refugee types from all the resettling going on there."

"I always pictured Mindanao as like the Wild West," I mused aloud. "They used to have Moslem fanatics there. They'd wrap themselves in thick vines and wander into a Christian village, or an American outpost, back when it was a colony of ours, and they'd wield a machete on anyone until you hacked them to death or shot them. Either way, it had to be enough to penetrate the vine armor they wore. Several centuries ago Mindanao was the center of a shrunken-head cult in the South China Sea. It wasn't until the advent of the Americans that headhunting finally stopped. It was also a center for the slave trade in this region."

"How do you know this stuff, Mississippi?" she asked me as the waiter delivered our orders.

"I don't know. Books, movies, legends."

"You read so much or something?"

"I like to read, yeah. Knowledge is power, you know. It's also entertaining. I was going to say it's erotic, but mixed company and all that."

"Erotic?" she asked with a chuckle. "Knowledge is erotic? Just what do you read? Maybe I don't want to know. Mixed company we are, like you said."

"I get chills when I learn things," I explained as I thought about what I'd just said. "Life seems bigger than life to me. Things that happen that make me notice, anyway. It seems sexual, it's so charged. I'll stick with 'entertaining' then, but that sounds so trite."

She shook her head as if trying to figure me out. "Neither did I think of knowledge as entertaining." She smiled between bites. "Maybe a love story or something, but not from a history book or whatever it is you read. Anyway, we'll be learning Tagalog, so I guess they speak it in Mindanao, or at least at our jobs. I'll be teaching English in some barrio high school, I found out. Actually, I was told that in the Philippines they call a barrio a *barangay*."

"And I'll be working for the regional offices of the Central Bank. It's owned by a cooperative, though. A cooperative of small farmers. I wonder how that works. And I'll be teaching computers—personal computers, desktops. I've never even seen one before."

"They don't have them in Mississippi?" she teased.

"They only had them anywhere the last few years. Who can afford one, and who wants to bother to learn?"

"Then how are you going to teach it to Filipinos if you don't know how yourself?" she asked. "If it's so hard to learn?"

"I didn't say it's hard to learn. They have manuals for them. I have a master's degree, and I know how to read manuals. I took a COBOL course as an undergraduate, and they must have seen it on my application to Peace Corps. I guess that's how they know I took COBOL, but I don't remember anything asked about this."

"They asked general things," Lois reminded. "You must have answered regarding something about your major. But didn't we give them our college transcripts too? That was so long ago, and they asked so many things, I don't remember anymore."

"I don't know. Anyway, that's something I'll be

doing. I don't know what the bank wants from me. And the same cooperative has a marketing branch for their products. I guess that means rice production. I don't know what else they grow."

"It's the tropics," she said. "It has a rainy season and a dry season. Unless where you're going has lots of irrigation, they grow something else besides rice in the summertime, I would think."

"Anyway, I'll be helping somehow with marketing, too."

"The music sure is loud," Lois complained. "Maybe we should move a few tables farther away from the stage. I can barely hear myself talk."

"Let's just listen," I suggested. "I like it. It's mostly folk. I like folk. Some of it's even country."

"Kenny Rogers?" she moaned.

"Yeah," I replied defiantly. "Yeah, I like Kenny Rogers."

"Mississippi would," she said, smiling.

"Where we'll be living, they call it our site," I said as if thinking out loud. "That's clever. Like logistics or something. Sounds military."

"Does it make you feel like you're back in the Marines? This guy here with me is from Vicksburg, Mississippi and is an ex-Marine. And I'm eating in a folk house in Manila, Philippines, with him, in the Peace Corps. Now you tell me how that happened and how something like that could ever happen?"

"A little ying and a little yang," I returned. "Makes the world go around."

"How do you know about the ying and the yang?" she asked in amazement.

"Us little hicks from the Deep South, huh?" I

snickered. "What do we know about anything except what the Klan teaches us? Right?"

"Well, not exactly the Klan," she answered, "you being Jewish and all."

"That must be it, then," I said looking at her and showing some of the disgust I felt. "The Jew in me somehow sucked some of that in from the Northerners we get. Where else could knowledge come from in a place like Mississippi?"

"You're being sarcastic," she said, embarrassed.

"Aw, naw."

Suddenly, the loudspeakers blared. It was more than Freddie Aguilar playing his guitar. It was a karaoke sound, and very intense. As he began his next song, the Filipinos in the crowd stood and cheered. More than cheered. They came unglued in a defiant celebration. *What was this song he was singing?* I wondered. It was magnetic. He quit playing his guitar altogether and let the sounds from the speaker accompany him as he used his hands to simulate a flow of tears from his eyes down his cheeks. Then he stood at attention with his fist clenched and placed over his heart as he looked up into the spotlight, which beamed on him as from an angel or even God. I could not get enough. Lois too was captivated. We quit eating and just watched, as did the other Americans in the room. Films of girls screaming for Elvis, or the Beatles, could not match the intensity and devotion these standing, hugging, and fist-clenching Filipinos displayed as they pounded the air with their fists in rhythm to the song. As the singer finished the last phrase, the exuberance of the crowd magnified even more.

As soon as the song and the cheering for it ceased,

a table of Filipinos behind us came over.

"Do not be frightened," they comforted. *I didn't think I was supposed to be*, I thought, as I smiled back at them. "We love Americans," one of them continued. "Do not let this concern you. We are just celebrating who we are. Free Filipinos. Not puppets of the Marcos dictatorship and his American masters. You are our friends. All Americans are our friends. It is just a pride we feel, knowing who we are as a people."

"I understand," I replied, even though I didn't, yet.

They seemed satisfied and returned to their table.

Lois and I looked at each other, bemused. The Marcos regime had been in power for almost twenty years and was corrupt, lethal, despotic. And hated by most of the country. The American administration had propped him up as part of our Cold War strategy. In the case of the Philippines, added American support was induced to keep our military bases on Filipino soil. But it was all coming to a head now, just as we arrived, ready to live among the downtrodden in a desolate area. I had joined the Marines hoping to fight in Vietnam. That did not occur. I had joined the Peace Corps to aid the poor and share cultures, and now I felt a confrontation that had the potential for war.

And what would happen to a single American girl? Lois, my new best friend. What did she face?

Later that night, back at the hotel, I told my director what had happened with Freddie Aguilar at the Hobbit House, and he explained it to me. The song Freddie sang that so energized the Filipino crowd was called "Ang Bayan Ko," or "My Country." Written against the American presence during colonization, it all but stood as the freedom fighter's national anthem, much like the song "Dixie" in Mississippi.

I can't say this didn't concern me, but mostly it excited me. This wasn't what I came here for, but it added to the allure. How could anyone be content back home, with life as usual, when there was a whole world around? A whole world I was now a part of.

Chapter 4

The best thing about training was that we got to see another part of the Philippines. Lois and I were sent to Zamboanga, in the southernmost tip of the island of Mindanao. Zamboanga lies on a peninsula. We were each put up by a host family for three months while we learned intensively the language—Tagalog, as we were told in Manila—something about Filipino culture and history, and more about who we would be working with when we became full-fledged Peace Corps volunteers.

Magellan was killed in the Philippines. I soon learned that in one of my history and culture classes. How did I not know that? But I didn't. He was killed by a chieftain named Lapu-lapu, sort of like Captain Cook was later killed in Hawaii. Magellan still got credit for circumnavigating the world, and for claiming the Philippines and other Pacific islands for Spain. Until he did this, the Philippines was made up of what we Westerners would call half-naked savages.

Before the advent of the Spanish, the encroachment of Islam was already changing the makeup of Philippine society, at least in part. Muslim traders sailed by boat as far as Southeast Asia, and, in the process of trade and cultural interaction, many they encountered converted to Islam. That's why Malaysia and Indonesia, for instance, are mostly Muslim to this day. As are the Philippine Islands south of Mindanao, as well as parts of Mindanao itself, which is the southernmost major island and the second largest island in the archipelago. With the coming of Catholic Spain, however, Mindanao suffered cultural tension that still exists. The remainder of the Philippines, those islands north of Mindanao, had little Muslim influence at the time of Magellan; it was open season for the Spanish missionaries and settlers that arrived.

In all this training, it was language that drove me crazy. While learning about the culture and history was very appealing, language and I do not get along. What made it worse was that after America drove the Spanish out of the Philippines in 1898, we were persuaded by the British to stay, in order to keep the Germans out. And even perhaps to potentially keep out the new upstart in the region, the Japanese. What that meant to me, besides more history that I loved, was that Filipinos also spoke English. They learned it in their schools after they adopted our school system, in their churches, and in their businesses, too. It became the unifying language for them, as did many colonizing languages for other countries that were subjected by European powers at the time. So, as I tried to converse with the locals and get down what little Tagalog I knew, they would reply in English. Either my speech was so atrocious, which I'm sure it was, or they wanted to show off to this new American in their midst how well they knew English. I never ever learned Tagalog. Period.

This was not the case for Lois, however. She took to Tagalog like a duck takes to water. Right in the middle of conversations she and I would have with locals, they would talk to her in Tagalog but to me in English, all in the same conversation.

The rest of our training was self-induced. Meaning we mingled where we wanted. This could be seeing a Tagalog movie at the local movie theater, or having a drink at a hotel bar, or perhaps sampling native cuisine in a restaurant somewhere.

But adventure called in the process.

"You can see Basilan from here," I said to Lois as we took a break after a cultural sensitivity class. The building where we trained was near the beach, and just beyond the bay you could see an island with palm trees.

"Sulu," Lois remarked, "is just past it. It's the main island, I suppose, of the Sulu Island chain. All Muslim."

"You want to go?" I asked her. "We could go either to Sulu Island in a tourist boat, or even one of these little crafts at the dock here that take people the few miles to Basilan. Just to see Moslem culture. And actually, Basilan is bigger than Sulu. It's the biggest island of the four hundred islands of the Sulu archipelago."

"Why do you call them Moslem?" she asked quizzically. "Is that what you say in Mississippi?"

"You make it sound racist," I commented.

"I don't guess it's racist, but you're the only one I hear calling them that."

"The o's and u's intermix in a lot of languages," I said.

"Somebody who struggles with language the way you do, and you notice something like that," she said with a chuckle.

"Knowing that is more in line with history than language. So I guess that's why."

"Isn't it dangerous on a Muslim island?" she asked.

"They're rather hostile here. And remember, it's a breath away from civil war here, and they've been at odds, often violently, since Christian settlers first began appearing. You're the one who told me about those assassins that wrapped themselves with vines and went hacking at the infidel."

"The Peace Corps wouldn't have put us in harm's way," I answered.

"That doesn't mean we have to tempt fate, though," Lois said. "And I'm a girl. I might be a little too tempting, don't you think?"

"It is just right there," I replied, pointing. "Surely Basilan is safe. Let's just bop there. Saturday's our last weekend here. It's now or never."

"And speaking of tempting fate," Lois chided, "you're not going to wear your Star of David pendant around your neck, are you? The Filipino Muslims on staff are taking it in stride, but they work for the Peace Corps. But it's bad enough just being a Jew around a lot of Muslims, so why do you flaunt it so much here? Thank God you don't wear your Israeli Defense Forces T-shirt here in Zamboanga like you did in San Diego, but still. You flaunt being a Jew. At first I thought it was some Mississippi thing. That you had defiance toward Southern bigotry or something. But I'd think you'd want to feel a little more secure while you're here."

"Security is boring," I replied as macho as possible. "But I'm not flaunting anything. The Peace Corps is supposed to be this culturally sensitive organization. We're supposed to share our culture while at the same time opening up, however much, to alien cultures and lifestyles. So here I am. A Jew among us.

I'm aware of my status in Mississippi. But most Jews, at least, have white skin and can blend in there, when we want. But it's not just Mississippi. For every three violent crimes against an ethnic group in America, two of them are directed at Jews. Not Blacks, not Latinos, not Indians, or Asians, but Jews. And everyone knows about the Holocaust, and the pogroms toward Jews in history, not to mention the Crusades. And all this about affirmative action now? Meaning quotas? Let minorities in universities even if they don't perform? Until World War II, Jews had quotas against them. To keep them out. To keep them from taking over law schools and medical schools. So I don't want to flaunt or rub anybody's nose into anything, but I just thought, while here, hey, y'all, here I am. A Jew. The Moslems on staff here are real good people. I don't know everything they think, but I go out of my way to be friends with them as a Jew, and they do the same to me."

I took a deep breath and stared Lois in the eyes. How was she handling my burst of passion, I wondered.

"I won't wear my pendant on Basilan," I promised. "Okay? So, are we going?"

"Okay," Lois agreed, rather fretfully. "I better not regret this."

"Hey, you two," someone said from behind us.

We turned to look.

"Hey yourself, Rhonda," Lois greeted.

With the girl named Rhonda were two other girls. They all had strong Yankee accents. Rhonda herself was from Rhode Island, while one of the girls came from Boston and one from Brooklyn in New York.

"Guess what we found out," Rhonda said

cheerfully. "All of us—me, Margaret, and Jenny here—found out that our sites are building us Nipa Huts to live in. I'm so excited. I'll have my own little cottage, even if it's one room, made out of bamboo and standing on stilts. No electricity or running water, but a new shelter, all my own. That's just the sweetest thing. They must be such good people where we're going."

"They must be excited to have an American in their midst," Margaret said. She was the one from Boston and was a middle-aged, gray-haired woman.

"When we all had our site visits," Jenny said, "our coworkers-to-be showed us around. They showed us where we'll be working, the agency and all, and are building our huts near there. I can hardly wait to go, now. All of us have the same story in that regard, even though we'll live in different communities."

"What do you do again, Rhonda?" I asked.

"I'm a registered nurse back in Providence, and my little town on Mindanao has a clinic next to the high school there. The hospital is in the provincial capital, but this village where I'm going is big enough that it has a clinic and a transient doctor. There are a couple of nurses there full time, and I'll be helping them."

I looked at her as if absorbing all she said, then turned to Margaret. Before I could ask about her situation, she began to explain to me about it.

"I'm working with the Department of Agriculture," she said smiling through her raspy voice and tobacco-stained teeth. "Now, how did an English Lit professor from Amherst get picked to live about a fourth the way up Mt. Apo with an agency that concentrates on forestry and erosion management? Someone explain that to me. But actually, I'm rather excited about it. I'll be living almost totally alone. I mean out in the countryside, not even in a barangay. But it couldn't be any more dangerous than Boston. The department head I'll be working with, and his family, lives next door, and it should be safe enough. I have a bowie knife, just in case. And some mace."

"I'll teach math at an elementary school," Jenny said, as if it was her turn to speak. "It's a desperately poor village, but the provincial capital is a jeepney ride away. I'll survive."

A jeepney is a Filipino contraption that derived from their imagination and old Army jeep parts left over from when the Americans ruled the Philippines. It's the major means of transport throughout the Philippines.

"You're going to be a teacher too, aren't you?" Margaret asked, looking at Lois.

"I'll teach English at a high school out in the barangay," Lois answered. "It's about an hour from Cotabato City, off the major highway, I have to take a jeepney down some dirt roads to get to my village. That's another hour. The village has a post office and a high school. Even a mayor's office. The buildings are in real dismal shape, though. It's very poor there. But they're building me a Nipa Hut. Same story as you guys. No running water or electricity either. We'll see how that works."

"An hour off the highway from Cotabato City, you say," Rhonda chimed with a wicked grin. "Rather convenient, wouldn't you say, Mississippi?"

I tried to keep a straight face, but burst out laughing. That was all the answer anyone needed. Their imaginations were salivating.

"Did you get a Nipa Hut built for you?" Jenny asked me.

"Naw. I live in town, right smack dab in Cotabato City, near the marketplace. That's where the bank is where I'll work. No Nipa Huts there. I found a retired high school history teacher who rents out rooms. She's ninety years old and has a big two-story house all to herself. I get a bedroom upstairs, and there's some college girls that share a room downstairs near her bedroom and the living room. They call her Lola."

"Aw, that's sweet," Rhonda said. " 'Lola' is like we'd say 'Granny' or something."

"Mr. Banker here," Margaret hooted at me. "You've got it rough. Near the marketplace, in a nice building. All the conveniences. Even sexy college girls."

"Chicks," Jenny said, making a small hiss as she did so.

They all glanced at Lois, who appeared unfazed.

"Well," I came back at them, "since you're already so jealous of my situation, let me tell you more. I'll have access to electricity, so I can have a fan in my room, and the bank has air conditioning. At least in the main office, one of those window units. And I get flown every two months, at the Central Bank's expense, to Manila to report what I'm doing."

"Oh, you're pathetic," Margaret howled. "How do you live with yourself? Spoiled brat! You better take us out when we come visit you in Cotabato City. Although, when I sow any wild oats, it's going to be in Davao. That's closer to where my site is. And it's the second largest city in the Philippines, so it might be the scene of some great escapes for us. But you'll be taking good care of Lois in Cotabato City, it sounds like, there, Mississippi. I'm sure of that."

"I'm sure he will," Rhonda and Jenny chided.

My shy grin helped me not blush from their implications.

****

Muslim boats in the Basilan strait between the island and Zamboanga City were unique. Lois and I often went to an oceanside bar just to feel the sea breeze and look at them as they sailed. Whole families made their livelihoods from fishing on them, and they often lived on them, as well. The sails were rectangular but usually were broader based at the bottom of the sail than at the top and often were variegated, with broad vertical stripes, each sail with its own colors.

Lois and I took a ferry boat on our last free Saturday, after classes, from the port farthest south of the city. I had a fascination with Muslim culture and was excited to see a pure setting. Being a Jew, I had visited Israel once, and went to a Muslim village while there. But it was small, and they seemed defensive in speaking with me. This would be different. I would be an American tourist visiting the local Muslims on their terms.

"They hold themselves differently," Lois said as we walked around the port area after we arrived in Basilan. "The Christian Filipinos are very nice people, but they seem to have an inferiority complex. Well, I don't know if that's fair. It may be something cultural about them that I'm not picking up. But the Muslims here have a pride about them. A better self-image. At least that's how it comes across to me."

"They are different here," I affirmed. "Maybe it's

just defiance. They got conquered by the Spanish, by the Christians, by the Americans, and again by Filipino Christians. They may just be in the mode of 'not going to take it anymore.' "

"Look at all the men smoking," Lois observed. "And beer sold. I don't know what I expected. More *sharia* or something. But they seem like anyone else except for their dress. All the skull caps. Skull caps are Jewish. What's a Moslem skull cap?"

"A Jewish skull cap is a *kippah*," I explained. "Yeah, I don't know what they call theirs. Do you want to talk to any of them?"

"I don't know," she replied. "I wouldn't know what to say. I'd feel like I'm on an interview or something. Let's just walk around."

"And we can't hold hands," I instructed. "They seem a bit relaxed for Moslem standards, but Moslems in the Middle East get pretty strict about their women. We don't want to flaunt our sexuality or freedoms any, just in case, you know."

"Okay, we'll act casual, and just walk around like naïve tourists, which we are, and if we see a shop or a café, we'll stop. Is that an agenda?"

I nodded my head as we headed toward the interior of the town.

I wanted something cultural to demand my attention. But it seemed a poorer and somewhat ethnically different version of Zamboanga. The only thing I was getting out of it was that I was doing it, as if satisfying some curiosity. In the Old City in Jerusalem, the Arab commercial stalls were so interesting. They had distinct character—*swarma* stands of exotic Arab cuisine, jewelry shops, water pipe shops, clothing stores. You could sit down and drink a cup of Turkish coffee and look at people wearing head dress or talking rapidly about something innervating. There was life and energy there. But now, in Basilan with Lois, I kept walking, just hoping I would stumble onto something that let me know what a Filipino Muslim was. Something especially different. Hopefully exotic.

"There's a café over there," Lois said. "Let's have a coffee."

I sighed and gave her a pronounced blink as a substitute for a nod.

It was a small outdoor café on the edge of a plaza. Café wasn't really the word to use, I determined, but it was close enough. It had only three tables, old, carved up, and wobbly. There was no menu, just a glass display nearby with a few food items.

"Coffee," we said in unison to the young waiter.

"I wonder where the mosque is," Lois said.

I shrugged, showing my boredom. The wheels started turning inside like they always did when I got bored. An entertainment to induce, no matter what.

"The Moslems were so much better to the Jews, in history, than the Christians were," I said to get conversation going.

I saw the expected look of surprise on Lois' face.

"They seem out to kill us all now," I said, to start off on a mutual point of reference. "But that's only since the advent of the state of Israel. I'm not too sympathetic with Moslem attitudes about Israel, but I understand it up to a point. The Holocaust was the last straw for Jews. If it had been the Holocaust and nothing else horrific to the Jews in history, there probably wouldn't be an Israel. But the Holocaust climaxed a tragic history. And it happened in modern times, with mass communication, so finally enough of the world felt enough pity, or regret, to support a Jewish homeland."

"The Nazis weren't Christian," Lois answered. "Can't pin that on Christians."

"Not pinning anything on anyone. Just talking. The Crusades were Christian."

"They were against the Muslims."

"Except that Jewish communities kept popping up on the way to the Holy Land," I intervened. "Some of the crusaders never made it to the Holy Land to drive the Moslems off. They spent a happy time wiping out the Jews on the way. Pogroms, Inquisitions, mass exiles of Jews by Christians. So then came the Holocaust, and now there's an Israel. But until then, I can't say it was a Jewish paradise in Moslem countries. We were definitely second-class citizens, with many restrictions, but there was at least a peaceful coexistence most of the time. We were simply a people to exploit like everyone else. The Moslems at their peak, right after Mohammed died, and with their empire expanded—man, those were glorious days for them, and often times even for their second-class citizens. The early Moslems were into science, the arts, math, philosophy. They revived Aristotle. And the Jews often thrived. But now there is hostility. If Jews had gone to Madagascar or South America or Uganda to start a Jewish state, there would have been trouble there, too. We still would have been intruding on someone. May as well intrude where things are historical and sacred to us. I don't know. I'm just talking, like I said."

"You know your history," a voice behind me said. I

turned around and smiled at a bearded, graying man standing near us at the edge of the plaza. "It is refreshing to hear a Westerner talk so kindly about Islam."

I nodded at him shyly.

"Oil wealth is all that is glamorous about Muslim countries anymore," the man explained. "There is so much to our history, and no one knows it. There is no oil here in the Philippines, so nothing seems glamorous. I suppose it is just hard times. But it is hard to be optimistic. Especially with Marcos in power. Are you American?"

"Yes, we are," Lois answered.

He nodded his head as if it explained something to him.

"Most Americans don't know anything about us," he said. "Just that we are backward and barbaric and uneducated. Perhaps I understand why others think that about us, but it is still not true. But it was good to hear your analysis, young man."

I nodded again in appreciation of the praise.

"What brings you here?" he asked further.

"We're in the Peace Corps," Lois answered. "Have you heard of it?"

"President Kennedy," he said. "Correct? Didn't he begin this organization? I knew there was Peace Corps in the Philippines, but I never met anyone before that was a part of it."

The waiter brought us our coffee, and I immediately paid him so that we could leave when we chose.

"What do you think of America supporting such a strong man as Marcos?" he asked, seemingly more from curiosity than to start a confrontation.

"We're not supposed to talk politics," I explained. "The world is complicated. Everything doesn't work out. I understand why you might be irritated with us."

The man stared off at nothing for a few minutes. "It is encouraging to me," he finally said, "that I met someone who knows something about us. I am appreciative of that."

He held out his hand in a friendly manner, and I shook it.

"I wish you well in our country. I have not met many Americans, and it makes me hopeful that we can work out our problems. *Salaam Aleikum*. I wish you well."

He turned to leave. Lois smiled at me approvingly. She instinctively reached over to touch my hand affectionately, but remembered my earlier warning, and withdrew it. It seemed worth our trip to Basilan to experience even this one conversation. It helped define why we had joined the Peace Corps, and it left us satisfied. We looked forward to becoming volunteers now. This felt like a graduation event toward that end.

Chapter 5

After our training was completed and we were designated full-fledged Peace Corps Volunteers, or PCVs, I was sent to my site in the capital of Region IX, Cotabato City, to begin my work out of the offices of the regional bank. The bank, as I'd learned while still in Manila, during processing, was small, owned cooperatively by local farmers, and included a marketing arm for their produce.

It was significant that I was assigned to this bank in this town, Cotabato City. It was also significant that I was trained, in the last three months, along with several other Peace Corps Volunteer prospects, in Zamboanga. Both of these cities were regional capitals of what had been, until now, no-man's land to foreigners.

Since the civil war between the Philippines and Filipino Muslim separatists, which began in 1971, almost all of Mindanao had a constant travel ban. No foreigners were allowed in. Our group was made up of the first foreigners officially allowed into these two semi-autonomous regions in over fourteen years. These so-called neutral areas were given a long leash, you might say, in running their own affairs, as part of a peace treaty. There were harsh restrictions beyond these neutral zones because the MNLF, Moro National Liberation Front, and the NPA, or New Peoples Army, which was a Communist-oriented revolutionary militia, still fought in this no-man's land.

Being a banker might sound important, but the word "Volunteer" that applied to the Peace Corps experience meant I didn't get paid much. Just enough to live at a middle-class level on the local economy, as was the case for all PCVs, including Lois, who as a high school English teacher made what I made. Middle class in a third-world country means meager, bordering on poor. This, in real terms, meant the equivalent of just under a hundred US dollars a month at the legal currency exchange rates at that time.

I liked Cotabato City. Everything's relative, of course. I'm sure if I'd been in Mississippi, which is not considered the bastion of modernity and prosperity in America, I would wonder what I was doing in a place that looked like pictures of the Great Depression. But Cotabato City was, by Philippine standards, a hub. The population was eighty thousand, so I was told. It had several universities, good transportation, supermarkets, restaurants, and even radio stations. It also had several banks besides the one I was assigned to. It had government agencies, which was important to me for projects to help out certain members of our bank clientele-ownership. And it had an airport. I could fly to Manila and a few other regional hubs on other islands. The major highway in Mindanao ran from Cotabato City, on one coast, east to Digos on the other coast. And being a coastal city, Cotabato City had access to several beaches, as well as a port from which I could access other port cities through oceanic transport.

I had never considered working in a city when I joined the Peace Corps, nor working for a bank. I'd wanted to work in the boondocks, which is a Filipino word meaning hillbilly country. But work is work, and there was work to be done, so I was game. In the Marine Corps we were taught to be riflemen first, no matter what our military job specialty was. In the Peace Corps we were to be good-will ambassadors first. So there was good will to exude and culture to share in a city environment. Rich and poor alike, city and barangay alike, all had an environment amenable to Peace Corps objectives.

Though I was the spoiled brat of my Peace Corps group, and just about everyone else's Peace Corps group, I was living a real Peace Corps experience. Living in a city, I had more expenses than the others, but the same salary. And I had skills to use with a larger clientele. I also had to learn how to use a personal computer so I could modernize part of the bank's operations and then teach the staff. I was on a different mission even if also the same mission.

My supervisor, the manager of the bank, was a Mr. Rancon, a middle-aged man with a degree in finance from a local university. He was friendly and seemed to welcome the idea of an American in his midst with a master's degree in economics. And a skill in computers, even though I didn't really have that.

Filipinos were short. At six foot, I was a head taller than almost every man I met, and the men weren't much taller than the women. In general, their hair was coarse and black and well kept. Their clothes were neatly pressed. I felt like a freak at times, not just from my height and skin color but from how my faded blue jeans and T-shirt were not pressed.

The one thing all PCVs were warned about concerned appearance. Besides the common sense of wearing clean, presentable clothes, we were told our T-shirts had to have a picture of some sort on the front, or at least some writing. Plain T-shirts were not culturally acceptable and were considered in poor taste. I wore flip-flops, what Filipinos called *tsinelas*. Foot attire wasn't covered, that I could remember, in the etiquette rules. Being American, white-skinned, and big, somehow lax clothing added to my mystique. I sure hoped so, anyway. Because I hated formal dress. Even semi-formal dress.

"This is James." Mr. Rancon introduced me to the bank staff during a special meeting upon my arrival. I felt almost human again, being called by my real name. "He is from Mississippi. The place in America with the strange-sounding name and spelling. He is an economist in America and will help us with our new computer that was given us by a US government agency. He will show us how to do stenography." Mr. Rancon looked toward, with a smile for emphasis, an attractive young girl, his secretary. He then looked at several other female staff and continued, "As well as how to store our bank records on a database. And also how to use this data on a spreadsheet. All these are new concepts to us, but it will help our bank keep track of our accounts better, and faster too."

Though I still wanted to learn Tagalog, it was a relief their English was so good. I understood every word he said. Now I always knew what was going on. At least the more obvious things. Their accents were very strong, but the English was understandable, and their sentence structure good. There was no reference point for me in their accents, though—they didn't sound Spanish, Chinese, Japanese, or anything I ever heard. More like from India than anything, but nothing at all like that either.

"James will attend *Samahang Nayon* meetings with me," Mr. Rancon said.

He saw the puzzled look on my face as he spoke and stopped to explain. "James, a Samahang Nayon is a village cooperative. Each area in our region has members that, together, have one vote as stockholders with our bank and marketing branch. They elect and hire. Within the cooperative, they help each other with savings and information. We report each month to them. You will join us in these meetings. Everyone has heard of our new American, and all are eager to meet you."

Filipinos are mild mannered and eager to please. They are sociable and friendly. Not just to a Hollywood-star-like American in the form of a Peace Corps Volunteer, but to each other. There can be duplicity and disgruntlement between them, but their intent is to get along, even to nurture each other.

My being a celebrity-like figure in their midst was even more pronounced in Mindanao. In Zamboanga, and here in my new home, people of Mindanao had been shut off from the rest of the world. Foreigners were new elements for almost everyone. We got huge amounts of attention here, even more than in other areas of the Philippines. Since Mindanao was treated like a military containment zone until now, under martial law, these people had been deprived of anything outside their village. This was in addition to their deprivations from war.

On my very first day at the bank, one woman explained to me, "Seeing you, an American, is the first sign of hope we have had after so many years of wars, hope that things are getting better. Maybe things will become normal here."

Lois told me a similar story in Zamboanga. A woman where she stayed cried at first, as Lois walked up to meet her. Lois thought that somehow the woman was frightened. When she asked what was wrong, the woman said, "Nothing is wrong. Just to see a foreigner again gives me hope all these years of isolation and bloodshed may be coming to an end."

But there is another side to the Filipino. Had to be.

Pacific Islanders, in general, and for sure Filipinos that I observed, could brood and hold onto grudges. It was important to watch one's words and the way those words were spoken. Something, however innocent, could be taken as slander. Americans, in their eyes, tended to be brutally frank. Me being Jewish, in an area with so many Muslims, made it even more important that I watched everything I did.

Cotabato City, by Philippine standards, and for sure Mindanao standards, was well off. The bank where I worked was one of the nicer buildings. But not even the bank could measure up to average housing in an American middle-class neighborhood. Our bank was made of wood and stone, had screens, fans, secure wooden doors, and cement flooring. But the paint was old and in some places peeling. The surroundings were dirty. Not profoundly so, but like an old country store back home.

Even Mr. Rancon didn't have an office. It was an office of sorts, and he often was the only one in it, but it was used for meetings, and shared by other bank officials. It had a window, with a cubicle air conditioner in that window, and there was an electric fan to help spread the cool air from the air conditioner throughout the room. The main lobby of the bank had, besides the screen doors, windows open with several ceiling fans throughout. It was rainy season now, which meant even more humidity than normal. In the Philippines, however, this humidity meant that as soon as it got very hot, rain would appear to freshen things. This kept even the lobby, with its staff and customers, comfortable. In the shade, if there was any breeze at all, the air felt refreshing.

A desk especially for me was placed in the room with Mr. Rancon. On my desk was the micro-computer. A Filipino clone of one. Next to it were a couple of boxes of five-inch blank diskettes, as well as packaged software for a word processor, a sequentially oriented database package, and a spreadsheet package. But there were no manuals for all this software. That concerned me.

I still had not told anyone I knew nothing about computers, but I did let them know I needed manuals in order to train people. I just left out the part about needing them for training myself first. After work, as Mr. Rancon and I walked to a *carinderia,* which is a small shack of a diner, for a beer, Mr. Rancon showed me a computer store. It was just a block over from the marketplace where the bus station and the bank were located. My heart sang.

PCVs learn quickly to access available resources. Since I was a city slicker while in the Philippines, I was one of those resources. Lois never failed to look me up when she came to town, which was usually once a week.

"I like your town, Mississippi." She smiled as we sipped a beer at my favorite carinderia. "A ceiling fan to sit under while drinking a cold one. It doesn't get better than this." She winked. "Have you ever had room temperature beer like we have in the barangay? Room temperature that's ninety degrees? I dream of sipping on a cold beer under a fan every night while I'm sweating to death on my hammock under my mosquito net in my Nipa Hut. I'm being rebellious even drinking a beer at all. Have you bothered to notice how women don't drink publicly in the Philippines? Even Imelda Marcos pours her beer into a Coke. That's what women do here, if they're bold enough to drink in public at all. You have to mix your beer with a Coke to keep from creating a scandal. But with you, Mississippi, the gloves are off. You and I are going to be beer-drinking buds and to hell with etiquette and Peace Corps good will for now. I need a break from all that, and I need a cold one."

"I don't know how it escaped me back home," I mused aloud, "how we were coming to the land of San Miguel."

"That's easy." She smiled. "You can't afford San Miguel Beer in Mississippi. In America it's an expensive import. Here, it's like a fountain drink."

"I'm making San Miguel my patron saint," I said. "Even though I'm Jewish and not Catholic. And what do you mean, we can't afford San Miguel in Mississippi?" I asked, rolling my eyes. "We're so poor or something? Ms. Ohio State grad with money hand over fist."

"Well, statistically speaking," she lectured, "the state of Mississippi is the poorest state in the country.

And, excuse me, but I have money? Me? I'm a product of the port of Cleveland. I couldn't have afforded a community college if I hadn't gotten a scholarship."

"You played a sport for Ohio State?"

"You're showing your machismo, Mississippi," she mocked. "I was valedictorian of my high school class and went on academic scholarship. And don't go thinking Peace Corps is all I can do, either, just because I'm an English major. I graduated summa cum laude. I get funded for Berkeley law school when I get out."

"You're going to Berkeley law school?" I asked. "Then why are you here?"

"Same thing you are, except living in a Nipa Hut while I do it, you spoiled-brat city slicker."

"No, seriously," I prodded her, "why did you join the Peace Corps if you've got all that going for you?"

"I wanted to see some of the world," she explained. "I want the Peace Corps to broaden my consciousness. I knew being stuck in one place most of my life would hamper my ability to perceive outside of the norm. I want to be able to conceive of a bigger picture and a bigger reality. We have to push ourselves. We can't get everything out of books alone, or by staying within the confines of the ivory tower of academia-type places. So, I want to sow some wild oats before getting bogged down with some law firm. Besides, it feels good helping others for a change instead of being some token woman in a corporate man's world. It's one of the things that attracted me to you, actually. You've been a Marine, and later you backpacked it around the world just for the sake of adventure. I like your energy."

"You used an interesting word, Lois," I said, smiling. "Are you attracted to me? I know you are. I knew from our encounters before. But you never say anything to indicate it openly. I like hearing it."

I saw her blush.

"Yeah, it's 1984," she explained. "Women are competitive now. We're lawyers and doctors and business moguls. I can tell a hunk of a man to his face that he puts flutters to my innerds. You're tall and muscular. You charm the dickens out of me. You're clever and a survivor type. You've been around. No one I'd rather sip a cool one with in the tropics. Does that answer you?"

I grinned and nodded. How could even a macho guy from Mississippi begrudge liberation of this nature for the opposite sex?

When together as volunteers at our sites, Lois and I slept in the same bed. We convinced ourselves it was platonic. Two lonely, best-friend Peace Corps Volunteers sharing the cruel world together. I had a slightly oversized bedspring in my room at my Lola's house that we placed a Filipino version of a mattress over. A straw woven mat. But at her place we shared a double-sized hammock.

Being a liberated Yankee woman, I assumed Lois felt at ease sharing a bed with a man, whether platonic or not. But she bothered to explain it to me that night as we lay next to one another in my bed at Lola's.

"Living in Mindanao," she said, "is a cultural and safety shock for me. It's leaving definite and deep marks of stress on me already. To combat this, when we're together in the same bed, I feel a comfort and a security with you. Somehow it repairs me a little. To even touch is so reassuring for me."

Whatever the reason, I welcomed it. And I didn't

want to feel like I was taking advantage of her, so I was glad this was her idea, even though it was mine. But I needed it too. Either because I was a typical disgusting male or because it helped comfort and reassure me too. From stresses or loneliness, I didn't know. I hadn't even thought about it until she brought it up. All the more reason to leave this as platonic as Mother Nature allowed. Meaning no sex. I went out of my way to make sure she didn't feel some obligation under which I might subconsciously pressure her somehow.

But.

I felt her body next to mine. I felt her body's warmth intertwined with mine. Slowly, through the weekends together, it happened. It wasn't platonic anymore. I tried pretending it was. Then tried not to think about it. But it got worse each time I saw Lois. I began to sneak wonderment at her expense and became like from another cosmos possessed. For as I gazed at her form, I understood why the obvious, pertinent, and daring features of her anatomical dowry allured. As well I should. But to look at the nape of her neck, and her cheeks, her chin, her rounded shoulders, her legs. Her lips. Those wonderful, precious, voluptuous lips. How could every square inch of everything about a girl be so tantalizing? So demanding. And ruthlessly so. I vaguely got that Mother Nature plays her tricks on us poor, unsuspecting, pathetically obedient creatures. But "keep doing it" was what I demanded back.

Keep trapping me and selling me your blandishments and appeals, I cajoled my tormentor, the above-mentioned Mother Nature. *For I am more than your victim in this matter. I'm your willing and beguiling accomplice in return. There is nothing more that I want from my life,* I decided, *than to be in blissful symmetry with your goddess-like anthropomorphic replenishment rituals and oblations.*

It got to where I dared Mother Nature on.

But there is a downside to women. God gets mischievous or something. A guy just can't have his cake and eat it too. Women like to shop. A lot. It drives me crazy. Lois drove me crazy. In her case, she could only shop when she came to see me. And also in her case, being a woman in a strange and sometimes dangerous setting, she needed a chaperone. Not only that, we didn't have that much time to spend together as it was. So that also forced my hand. I had to shop with her in order to be together with her. To her, shopping was pure joy and entertainment. Her joy was the only thing I got out of shopping with her, though. For I hated shopping. Hugely so.

"Clothes here are made locally," she informed me, oblivious to my displays of complete boredom. "Either that or imported from China." One by one she would pick up a muu-muu, if that's what it was, or a pair of slacks, to inspect them. As if it mattered. Somehow it always mattered to women. "There is nothing Western in any of this I've seen." She looked up at me as if to emphasize the importance of her findings. I smiled just enough to show her I was trying to care. "Not just here," she continued, "but in every market clothing booth I've been to."

One at a time she inspected more items. There were no shoes at this particular shopping area, so I had hope this would not go on forever. She, like me, was wearing *tsinelas*, so maybe she was satisfied with these. But I was damn glad I didn't have to press my luck and find out.

She held up another piece of dress I called a muu-muu. "Barrio busters is what I call these shifts," she said, not looking up from the dress. I was grateful when she kept inspecting these items so I didn't have to force another smile. "This is what all the local women wear," she continued, "except for the Muslim women. This and capri pants."

Things worked out after we got home, however. One by one she would try on what she'd gotten. In front of me. And as I began to understand that, I liked her shopping sprees more and more all the time.

Chapter 6

No matter how many Samahang Nayon meetings I went to, I never knew what they were talking about. I still didn't know Tagalog. Mindanao, in Filipino demography, was indeed the Wild West. As we learned in training, Mindanao was Muslim until the Spanish arrived. It was settled through the centuries by Christian settlers from provinces from all over. Tagalog and English were the unifying languages. For those that resented Tagalog for being the dialect from Manila, English was preferred. But at these bank meetings, a Filipino language was used. Meaning Tagalog. Meaning too bad for me.

I was brought along because I was a showpiece. An American. Hollywood. It helped attendance. Not only that, I could sing. Filipinos are a musical people. Not all sing well, some even seemed tone deaf. But they loved to sing. Even the tone deaf bellowed out when they sang. Somewhere along the line, every get-together had singing in it, and being American, I was the one they had to hear.

But I was from the South. We're musical too. Not every Southerner is as bold as a Filipino, but singing is old hat, nevertheless. I felt self-conscious when they first zeroed in on me, but I looked forward to every time thereafter.

"We must enter you in a contest, James," the

Samahang Nayon chairman said. "They have them in Cotabato City." He looked at Mr. Rancon. "You must enter him. Advertise he is from our bank. That may help with deposits. He is good enough to win."

"Sing us one more," a wrinkled old lady said.

"Yes, sing for us, James," Mr. Rancon seconded.

I could tell my boss was proud of me.

A middle-aged man in *tsinelas*, worn cotton shirt, and disfigured straw hat brought me a guitar. The strings were stiff and partially corroded, and there was a large hole toward the bottom of it. I wasn't good with the guitar, but I preferred even this to *a cappella*, as was usually the setting when I sang.

I strummed the chord of G. It was out of tune. The metal screws to tighten the strings at the head of the guitar were rusty, so I gave up even the thought of trying to get it in tune.

I strummed the strings again as an introduction to the song "Old Shep." This was a favorite in Mississippi. I was certain Filipinos didn't know this song, but it was sentimental, with a pretty melody, and easily recognizable about a little dog. Everyone loved dogs.

The song brought smiles. As I finished they were ready to ask for more, but Mr. Rancon intervened.

"We must return to the bank," he apologized. "Please let our friend James eat his dinner, so we can get back to our duties."

"Here, James," the chairman said, handing me a banana leaf laden with rice and grilled native catfish.

The native catfish could be found abundantly in the streams nearby. They were small in comparison to the catfish back home, but even these were a luxury here. They were collected and prepared for a communal gathering such as now. Even better tasting was an air-breathing predator fish called Dalag. They were bigger, and a pest, the way they skimmed in rain water from one fish pond to another, or one rice paddy to another, and ate the local fish, then escaped. But they tasted like perch did back home, or perhaps better.

Most poor Filipinos ate only rice for a meal. At times, it was supplemented by a green native bean the size of a BB, called *mongo*. Mongo was high in plant protein and was called the poor man's steak. Occasionally, a farmer would kill one of his chickens for the full animal protein content. Native chickens ran around freely and should have provided a meal for an entire family. But they were testimony to the scarcity of any kind of food supply. They were skin and feathers. When one was killed, a few handfuls of meat was all that was provided. The locals claimed they had more flavor than the fat American chickens. But I decided they were being as optimistic as they could manage about the situation they were in. And in a Filipino's case, they grilled or made a soup out of the claws and head, in addition.

Everything got eaten in the Philippines. Food was too scarce. I looked around and saw a pig so skinny its ribs stuck out.

"Come, James," Mr. Rancon said while looking past the highway in front of us. "We must leave now or the rains will reach us."

Dark storm clouds had appeared at the horizon. They seemed miles away, but everyone was concerned by them and hurried to clear the area, leaving.

A little puppy meandered over to me as if to say goodbye to the American. Like the Chinese I'd heard about, Filipinos eat dog. So how was this one still alive, I wondered. How had it not yet been eaten?

As we hurried to the jeep to take us back to Cotabato City, I turned one last time to look at the puppy.

"You're next," I said toward the pup fretfully, concerned for its survival.

This Samahang Nayon we were leaving now was not so far from the village where Lois lived. I yearned to ask the bank to leave me somewhere near her and I would gladly find my own way back. But it was the middle of the week, and I would have to miss work to do so, since it took so long to get to Cotabato City with public transportation, namely a jeepney. Disappointing as it was to miss seeing her after being so close to her village, still Lois and I had already agreed to meet at her place the coming weekend.

I liked visiting Lois, I thought to myself on the way to Alamada that next Saturday. Nothing was as entertaining as this ride. For whatever reason, Alamada was considered the Wild West of Mindanao. Since Mindanao was considered the Wild West of the Philippines, why were they sticking a single, white-skinned female Peace Corps Volunteer, namely Lois, out there? And she wasn't in Alamada itself, but in one of the villages a jeepney ride away.

It didn't seem dangerous to me, going there. I didn't doubt the danger, but never saw it. And the locals insisted it was as safe as any place around. Which wasn't saying much. I assumed its remoteness worried people and they accepted such worry as a way of life.

The national highway from Cotabato City to Digos was in reality a two-lane street. It was paved. Except for the many potholes. That's the most you could say for it. After the national highway portion of the trip was completed, the road to Alamada itself—and I mean road as in narrow dirt road—went north. We had to pass by and through parts of rain forests. That's why I liked this trek. A ride through the tropics at its best. At its wildest best, unless going on foot, or by *carabao*, which is the native water buffalo.

A jeepney is more than the primary means of transportation in the Philippines. It's the transportation bloodstream of the Philippines. The front of one looks like a jeep, from which it originally derived, but joined as one unit with a body not much longer than a Volkswagen van. It is usually silver or gray in color but with different paintings and slogans on it to make it personal to the company or person owning it. There are no windows. Just open space where windows belong, with bars to provide support for the goods people stuff on these things. Tied to the bumpers at front and rear, and on top of the roof, were water jugs, bags of rice, chickens, pigs, bamboo slats, and anything else someone might need. The animals weren't just tied, they were strapped upside down, with parts of them hanging over the edges.

When a Filipino arrived at his hut, he would tap on the side of the jeepney, accompanying that with a kissing sound to get the driver's attention. After letting the passenger off, along with his possessions, often the jeepney would have just begun to pick up speed when yet another passenger tapped and mocked a kiss to get it to stop again. This aspect drove me crazy. The distance between stops was often only a few yards. Filipinos hate walking, especially in the dust and heat, but I determined this was also a grab at what pride they could muster in their poor existence, with a stop made just for them alone. At least the ride to Alamada was remote enough that we didn't have very many stops along the way.

Halfway along on the trip we crossed a small river, perhaps really a large stream. There was an ancient-looking, rotting embodiment of a structure that surely was a bridge at one time. The only thing that allowed us to cross anymore was a fallen coconut tree laid across this small river. When I say we crossed a river, I don't mean by jeepney. Passengers had to disembark, untie their belongings, including said chickens, pigs, and supplies, manage them across the coconut tree bridge, then load them again onto a waiting jeepney on the other side of the river to continue their journey. It was irritating, but entertaining. I'm sure my entertainment was only because I seldom came this way, only at times like now to see Lois. It made me feel special that Lois endured this adventure once a week just to see me. Of course, I was keenly aware she also came to see Cotabato City itself, which seemed like Paris, France, to her, I was sure.

I seldom saw more than the marketplace and the jeepney depot of Alamada. Cotabato City had a bus station and even an airport, but Alamada had one small center for transportation, and that was it. This was not just the hub for jeepneys but for tricycles, as well. Tricycles were motorcycles expanded into three-wheeled taxis. Even moderate-sized villages had these. Behind the handlebars was the typical narrow, plastic-covered seat that the driver straddled. Attached solidly behind the seat of the tricycle was an open compartment with seats that held two passengers.

The times I visited Lois' village, it was too far for me to affordably hire one of these tricycles. So I would find my jeepney, squeeze on it, and wait to be driven. Often times I couldn't even squeeze onto a jeepney. I shared a ride with other Filipinos, their livestock and goods, so resorted to standing on the bumpers, or even riding on the roof like many of them did. Women were never allowed to ride outside. Too dangerous. Not just because they might fall off, but it tempted fate for an ambush, also. Before long, as if on a shift change at a factory, the jeepney would stop. Those riding the bumpers got inside, and men from inside would take their place. *I will be the one*, a Filipino would say as he tapped the man he replaced on the shoulder when taking the ride outside. He now took the risks and endured the hardships. The barangay version of *Noblesse Oblige.* The strong protecting the weak in this third world setting of knights of the round table.

In this part of the world, no one had seen a white man before. Probably ever, even before the civil war. No one seemed ashamed to stare at me, no matter where I went. The youth, especially, accompanied the stares with a "Hey, Joe," which derived from the time when American soldiers occupied the Philippines as our one and only colony in history. An American soldier was a G.I. Joe, and then just Joe. So now, it was a "Hey, Joe" everywhere I went. Sometimes kids would walk up to me just to touch my skin, as if to see what I was made of. Since I was a Peace Corps Volunteer, ambassador at large, I usually smiled and acknowledged them. But many of these kids liked to show off and insisted on getting my attention constantly. I burned out eventually, somewhere along the line, and ignored them, even putting on my cassette player to listen to music loudly through earplugs. *Stay away*, my mood said as I thought back to all the weeks I was patient with this treatment before my burnout.

It was early afternoon when I finally arrived at Lois' village. That was okay, since schools in the Philippines held session on Saturday mornings. At least now she had time for me.

That Filipino schools held session on Saturday morning sounds impressive, as if education was taken seriously. But they only had ten grades. Six elementary school grades, then no middle school, but straight to four years of high school. And village schools were usually of low quality. Kids had to work in the fields with their parents. And any Filipino who had college education at all stayed out of impoverished villages, even their own. All the more reason the Peace Corps volunteered to help fill in the gaps.

Lois knew I was coming, and I saw her leaning out of her window looking for me. My heart leapt. No other way to put it. There she was, and there she was looking for me, for no one else but me. And I was here. When she finally saw me and I beheld her wide smile and exaggerated wave, I wanted to run to her. *How the hell did I let this happen to me?* To be so excited to see a girl I couldn't have. I was sure she wanted me just as much, and also sure that assessment didn't derive from my ego or from longing. Everything about her exuded how much she wanted me. The problem was, *What the hell were we going to do about it?* We still had not fully come to grips with the fact of our wanting. The fact of a hoped-for "us."

She held the door to her Nipa Hut open for me as I climbed the bamboo ladder to her one-room studio-sized apartment. There was a longing inside me for a hug, even a kiss, but the momentum of our platonic past kept it from happening.

Her Nipa Hut stood on the edge of the village, adjacent to the home of the school principal and his family, since she was a lone white American woman. For her security. The Peace Corps insisted she live with a family, but she had found a way to attain her Nipa Hut. In a family setting, members of a household could enter her surroundings and premises at will. Not just from curiosity but for the security concern, as well. And since Filipinos are social to the point of loathing ever to be alone, in their eyes, everyone in the universe wanted eternal companionship. At all times Filipinos had a *kasama,* or chaperone. By choice. To be alone at any time seemed punishment by solitary confinement to them. Which was another reason Lois insisted on her own Nipa Hut. Privacy. She wanted to be able to escape to privacy somewhere in her village existence, and not have to concoct excuses to find a way to have her sacred aloneness.

No electricity or running water was anywhere to be found in this village. Big cities like Cotabato City had electricity in half or more of the municipality, but not so in these remote rural villages. Luxuries like that didn't exist except in comic books. The shower in Lois' Nipa Hut was a small hole in the floor, partitioned off by walls made of palm leaves to create a space the size of a small closet. The shower spout, so to speak, was a coffee can dipped into a bucket of water and poured by hand. The toilet was similar, but with a plastic container beneath the floor on the ground to collect the night soil. Her "kitchen" was similarly primitive: she cooked by placing coconut shell charcoal in a metal pot with a grill over it. The most modern convenience, perhaps, in her entire hut was the kerosene lamps she had spread throughout.

"You're just in time," Lois told me, grabbing my hand to lead me back out after I placed my small backpack onto her one table. "I have to collect water before dark. We'll do it now, if you don't mind."

A road led to the only hand water pump her side of town used. Her impatience, however, sought out any shortcut she could find, which included walking through rice paddies. Paddies were bordered with dikes to hold in the flooding required by the rice plants. The dikes were built to a foot or so above water level and were about a foot across, for a path. It was a trick to walk them in *tsinelas*, but for Lois, carrying a two-gallon jug of water in each hand, and me, with bigger jugs of five gallons each, it was even trickier. These dikes were especially hard to negotiate when we got tired, which happened a lot with all the water we carried. We had to make it to the end of a rice paddy before we could set the jugs down to rest. With each rest stop we felt an inner sigh of relief at our successful journey across the last one.

"How do you manage?" I asked when we got back to her hut. "If you can carry only four gallons at a time, that doesn't allow you much water."

"I have to go every other day," she explained. "But those two boys I'm tutoring help me sometimes, too. I manage. Other people help sometimes. They love their American here."

I nodded as I thought about it. I could picture it more than I could understand it.

"Mississippi, I need you to come with me." We had placed the water jugs in a corner near her sink area. "I'm part of a committee in this village that is meeting with an organization from Australia. They are from an agency, something akin to our USAID. You know what that is, right? The US Agency for International Development."

"Of course I know USAID, Lois." I grimaced while wrinkling my brow to show how my intelligence felt insulted.

"Sorry, sorry!" She smiled. "Just making sure. Anyway, this agency from Australia is here to give money for an earthen dam on the small river nearby. With that the village can regulate irrigation. Right now they are totally dependent on rain for their crops. If they could have irrigation, they could have an extra harvest of rice every year. Imagine that, almost doubling their income every year. They could still get in a planting of mongo beans in between. I think I heard that. But rice is the cash crop, and that would boost their income. Instead of almost starving to death, they'd be up to horrifically poor. I'm sounding like an economist, aren't I? I guess you're rubbing off on me. Anyway, come with me. Maybe you could even advise us. We have to leave now, though. That's why I'm in such a hurry. The meeting is near the school, in the mayor's office. We're almost late."

My smile was my answer, and again she grabbed my hand and pulled me out of her Nipa Hut.

Lois' village was small, but still larger than what we call a small town in Mississippi. The few real houses in it were small wooden structures. They were the local version of mansions for the rich. Mostly, the village consisted of coconut trees intermingled with Nipa Huts. No shops to speak of, just feeble structures about five feet square that sold cloth, or canned goods, or perhaps a simple cooked meal.

A cleared space was in the middle of the village, approximately the size of a tennis court. This was used as a solar dryer, where farm produce such as rice, mongo beans, or fish was spread over a hard cement surface to be dried by the sun. In between harvests the area was used as a basketball court.

The high school where Lois taught was on the way to the mayor's house. It was the most solid structure in town, even more so than the town hall where we headed. Both structures were wooden. The high school also took the most space, as much as the solar dryer and town hall combined.

The mayor was short and pudgy and looked to be in his forties. He was also a farmer, owning more than twenty acres, which was a big farm by village standards. He also owned the town's only jeepney and several tricycles. His house was the biggest in the village, containing four bedrooms. His clothing indicated his standing in the community: a starched blue cotton dress shirt that had a collar, black slacks, and; instead of *tsinelas*, black leather shoes that laced.

The two Australian officials were tall, athletic-looking men in their thirties. They were friendly, but blunt.

"We've helped your village out before, Mr. Mayor," the taller of the two said. "It is an impoverished village that we sincerely want to help."

I loved their accents. To the untrained ear it sounds British. But soon the twang becomes evident, similar to that heard in the pop song of the sixties, "Tie Me Kangaroo Down." I wanted to snicker but behaved myself, sure they felt the same way about my strong Southern accent.

"But," the other Aussie added, "we have a problem with this village. It seems we want to help you more than you want to help yourselves. This is a loan, not a grant. It is a loan because we need to see signs of accountability. We want to invest this loan and use the proceeds for future investments and loans to help other areas. It is one thing to be poor, but another to insist on staying poor. You will never pull yourselves up without responsible fiscal management. We gave a grant to your village for your solar dryer. But half the money was kept by a previous mayor, who chose to improve his personal lodging with it."

The present mayor squirmed.

"That mayor is gone now," the present mayor said. "I can assure you we will not allow corruption."

"Your solar dryer is half the size for which we gave you money," the first Aussie said. "Then we provided a loan for your school, and again, it was a loan so that we could hold you more accountable. But much of that money was not paid back by your citizens. Of the money siphoned off, most was shared for personal use by several of your village leaders. They were not invited to this meeting. We want to help your village. You desperately need the extra income this earthen dam would provide. The loan can greatly enrich your community. But it is the last offer our agency will give you. This is your last chance, as far as we're concerned."

"I totally understand you," the mayor said. "I will hold a meeting with all our village leaders, and we will sign an oath, a contract, to return with interest all the money in the loan."

The men looked the mayor square in the eyes, then reached out to shake his hand as a sign of faith.

"When we see the contract signed," the original Aussie spokesman said, "we will most probably provide the money for you. Thank you for your understanding."

"Thank you, sir," the mayor said. "You will notice I have two American witnesses with us. This gentleman here works with the Central Bank of the Philippines. We have him here to assure you."

I did not want to spoil the show, but hearing this made me feel uneasy, even with knowing I wasn't legally responsible for anything. I looked cynically at Lois, thinking she had divulged this information about me to the mayor. She smiled at me sheepishly.

"I'm sorry," she said as we arrived back at her hut. "I barely remember mentioning to the mayor you were coming. He already knew you worked for the Central Bank, from conversations past. You looked like you wanted to strangle me. Are we still friends, Mississippi?"

"I did feel on the spot, Lois. I know you didn't mean to get me involved."

"So, we're still friends? You're not afraid to visit me here anymore?"

The smile appeared on my face before I knew it was there. She was vulnerable to me. I liked that. It seemed worth it now, the encounter with the mayor.

"But you know," she continued, knowing I was

okay about things, "as poor as this village is, why are the Australians worried about a few thousand dollars when these people are desperate?"

"Because they need to learn accountability," I said, point blank. "And like the Aussies said, whether you see them as rich or not, it is an investment that could be used for other projects. Opportunity costs, an economist would say. The poverty is massive here. More accountability is required, more resources need to be renewed, and more projects need to be fulfilled. So I agree with the agency. It's one thing to help people. It's another to just pour money down a sewer and reinforce their mindset of taking. Taking responsibility for yourself is the first step to getting on your feet. These villagers have a hard life. Here's a chance to pull themselves up. But it comes with a cost, and I don't mean the interest on the loan. I mean responsibility."

"You sound just like the International Monetary Fund," she bit out.

"Yeah, well, I hope so," I hit back. "The IMF is vilified for giving bankrupt third world countries a chance, and corrupt governments keep defaulting on the loans."

"They are desperate countries," she sneered.

"Not their dictators. Their dictators pocket it for personal gain and despotic power building. For bribes. For goons and guns to oppress their people. The IMF knows this and doesn't intend to be held hostage just because liberals like thinking they have a monopoly in caring for the poor."

She stared at me. It wasn't hateful, but she didn't seem happy with me.

"You aren't doing anyone a favor by letting them

slouch, Lois."

"You are such a Southern redneck."

"That ain't redneck. That's me wanting to help people."

She studied me for a second, then reached up and touched me on the cheek. Her expression mellowed as she did so.

"I believe you, my darling," she said softly. "I think you really mean it. You aren't a redneck nor a Shylock. You're the kindest, dearest, most caring man. You belong in the Peace Corps with me. We'll get our job done with these people together."

I looked at her as if I could see inside her. "You called me 'darling' just now," I said. "I know in an endearing, not-to-be-overstated manner. But not too long ago you openly said you were attracted to me, and now I hear 'darling' from you. My hormones are exploding now. I'm just warning you. I don't want to make a fool of myself."

"It wasn't a Freudian slip, and it was beyond an endearment, Mississippi. I repeat, you're the dearest person I've ever met. You're rubbing off on me, and I love it. You've the biggest heart of any friend, so-called liberal, or church cohort I ever had. Take it any way you hear it." She stared at me for emphasis. "Darling mine."

A tear formed at the corner of one of my eyes, and it embarrassed me. "Do you suppose we're falling for one another?" I asked, surprised it came out so easily.

"That's exactly what it means," she replied. She rubbed at the moistness by my eye with a fingertip, then placed it on the edge of the upper part of her lip to savor like honey. She then moved her hand gently to the back of my neck to pull me toward her. We kissed. How precious the first moist, warm kiss, knowing that on the other side of it was a soul and feelings. We held to each other while savoring our passion.

"Supper can wait," I suggested. "What I want to do is shower together, then go straight to bed."

A deeper kiss was her response.

"I shutter the windows and tie them down at night," she said. "That and bolt the doors. Just in case somewhere during the night some adventurer gets greedy for my goods. Meaning me. But with you here, I feel secure. And it'll be too hot with everything shut. It'll be especially hot in each other's embrace."

I looked over at her hammock. "How will we make love in that?" I asked.

"You'll see," she replied. "Because I swear, we're going to find out."

Chapter 7

I watched Mr. Rancon's secretary struggle as she rewrote the entire manuscript containing the minutes of the meeting we'd just had. One little change seemed to require an entire rewrite. Maybe this was the break I was looking for with her.

She grimaced as she watched me walk over to her.

"I can help you with that," I said.

"I'm too busy," she replied sharply.

She was always too busy. Everyone in the whole bank was too busy for me to help them learn what could be done more simply and systematically.

I pointed to her change, the one I had just seen her make.

"I could put that beginning marker I showed you last week," I said calmly and professionally, hoping it would trigger something in her psyche besides feeling harassed, "and then the end marker, and move that entire paragraph anywhere you want it. That's what I was doing last week in my demonstration of the word processor. I know it doesn't make sense. Things never make sense in the beginning. I could also insert the change you just made right smack dab in the middle of that paragraph, and the paragraph would adjust to the change." I looked at her and grinned, hoping to lighten her up. "You were just too busy hating my guts, before, to see what I was doing."

She almost smiled.

Filipino cultural etiquette reflects eastern Asian etiquette norms in that everyone has to have what's called in Tagalog *paki-sama*. *Paki* means pleasing. *Sama* means together. In "pleasing-together" there is a lot of emphasis on saving face, which makes it hard to get things done if something runs counter to this saving-face form of etiquette. In fact, things often don't get done at all because of it. Being blunt is too impolite in Filipino culture, where everything gets phrased to avoid displeasure. An American sees this as silly and childish. But that's why Filipinos often talk to one another in more strained detail than what Americans put up with. This is to smooth out the way, to make sure things are done just so. Americans, in terms of sensitivity to others, can be quite crude. This is exactly why I often mixed the two styles. Bluntness to shock them into paying attention, and exaggerated concern or flattery, perhaps humor, to smooth it out for them to respond favorably. Otherwise it's just seen as scandal.

"I'll do this for you if you let me," I told our secretary. "I promise. You won't have to lift another finger. If you don't let me, you'll have to rewrite this entire page. Please, this one time, give me a shot. I won't instruct you, or get in your way. I'll do it for you."

She wasn't convinced, but after thinking about it for a moment, she got out of her chair and let me behind the computer, which now had been moved next to the typewriter at her desk.

As she sat in the chair next to me, she leaned as far away from me as the back of her chair allowed. I hoped she would find something else to do, to limit the chance of her being intimidated again by the modern age machine I kept forcing down her throat. But she sat there, and slowly the sneer she wore turned to boredom.

She was pretty when she wasn't hating my guts. Especially in the new blue-and-white square-patched dress the bank gave all the female employees as a uniform. She and one of the bank's agricultural consultants had just gotten married. He was one of the few Filipinos bigger than me, and he thought he could take me physically. I knew this because he was ready to spar with me a couple of weeks before, for fun supposedly. I wasn't sure, though, if it wasn't to check out an American, an American Marine to be exact, or because his girlfriend had me on her most-hated list lately.

"Look," I said to her, smiling. "I have the entire manuscript done for you on the computer screen here."

"You left out the change Mr. Rancon just added," she replied.

"No, I didn't. I'm going to do it now. To show you how all the time you've been hating my guts was a waste."

I saw her squirm from embarrassment.

Pow, just like that, the new sentence from Mr. Rancon was inserted into the manuscript. Her eyes lit up. I had shown her how to do it before, but instructed her at it then. She was so frustrated and upset with me for intruding on her duties she had obviously missed what I was getting at. But there it was now, and I had done it, not her. She saw it, and I knew I scored some points.

"Now, I'll just save this file, and you'll have it on diskette to use anytime you need. To make further changes or to print yet again. What shall we call the file?"

"What do you mean?" she asked. "What file are you talking about?"

"What I just did. This letter or report. Let's give it a name, and it will store electronically on this floppy diskette I'm putting in the computer now."

"Okay," she said.

"Come on," I coaxed. "Give a name that will make sense to you. Eight characters. MT101184. MT stands for meeting, and then today's date."

"I know that," she said, smiling. "I figured it out."

"And you'll figure the rest of it out, too," I promised her.

"Okay, call it that," she said. "And show me how to print it on our printer."

I showed her which icon to electronically access to save the file and then the simple steps to print it. As the manuscript came out on paper, her eyes lit up again.

"You'll have to tear off the perforated edges of the paper with the holes," I explained. "But then it's just like regular typewriter paper, except for a few little strands maybe."

She inspected the paper and shook her head in disbelief. I had finally won with a staff member about this computer. I lived to see the day. Maybe now she would tell the other girls I trained in the spreadsheet or database organizer. I knew nothing was going to change things with them, but then, I'd thought that with the secretary, also.

It was a good way to end my day. On a positive note, as they say. I didn't always get positive notes, so I grabbed this one, and made my way home.

I was in the mood for a San Miguel at my favorite local little carinderia but was already running out of money, even though it was only the middle of the month. There was always something to buy, usually for a project I was undertaking. Diskettes, manuals, bee supplies, tilapia fingerlings. So I decided I had to discipline myself and stay home, not spend anything. Lois was coming this weekend. We didn't do much, but I wanted money to do something while she was here.

My Lola was always entertaining. I needed nothing else to make my spare time pass happily by if I just came home to her. I still could not believe she was ninety years old. She was more spry than I was. The gray head of hair she wore gave away her age, along with the way her midsized frame was slightly bent. She had a few age spots on her skin, but with her energy and wit there was a feeling of youth about her.

"You can have the small stove, Mississippi," she said to me in her kitchen. "The wood-burning one."

My real name of James didn't survive with her past the first weekend Lois visited us. As soon as my Lola heard me addressed by Lois with my Peace Corps nickname, and understood the significance and humor of it, then Mississippi I was from then on. Even the college girls I boarded with picked up on it, to please my Lola, if nothing else.

"They're both wood burning," I replied.

"Yes, I know," she said, "but we usually use *ipil-ipil* for the big stove."

Ipil-ipil is a small native tree in the Philippines that is common and abundant. It not only is a good source of fuel for fires, but also is high in producing nitrogen in the soil, meaning a good source of natural fertilizer.

"That's what we use in the small stove too," I reminded her.

"You know what I mean, Mississippi." She sighed.

I thought about nodding agreement that I did understand, but I too blatantly didn't have a clue what she was getting at, so I just stared instead.

I heard rustling from the big stove on the other side of the room, where my Lola prepared supper for herself and the girls. I turned to look at what was happening.

"I may need your help." She grinned at me when she saw my curiosity. "I'm ready to boil alive an octopus. It is half dead now, but when I put it in the boiling water it will resurrect. I have the pot lid, but if it fights hard, you may want to help me."

I knew to take her seriously. Somehow she really did have a half-dead octopus she was going to wrestle with. She bent over to pick up a straw-mat basket-type bag, then glanced at me once again before laughing. Slowly, she placed the straw bag containing the octopus over the large pot of boiling water and began to tilt it.

"Here goes," she said. "Can you come just in case?" she asked me.

I walked over to her, but stayed slightly behind. She dumped the contents of the bag over the water, and I watched a large clump of tentacled clay-like substance fall into the pot. Immediately, the large tentacles jerked past the pot edge. I saw the slimey suckers. The octopus jerked, trying to get out, but my Lola had the pot lid ready and slammed it on top of the creature. It struggled violently for a moment, went limp, and sank. My Lola kept the lid forced on it for another minute to be sure.

"Would you like some, Mississippi?" she asked me as she began to add spices and pour in rice.

"It's not kosher," I answered. "As far as seafood goes, Jews can only eat fish with scales and fins. Octopus is off limits."

"I have seen you eat prawns," she corrected.

"Only under laboratory conditions, Lola," I replied with a grin.

"Oh, you are as bad as Christians," she said, chuckling. "Rules are made to be broken. I have to remember that the next time I break a vow. I am doing this under laboratory conditions," she said as if learning the words by heart.

"What is happening, Lola?" one of the college boarders inquired as she entered the kitchen. Soon the other female boarders followed her.

They were so young. College students in the Philippines are younger than American college youth in years, but they looked so young even beyond that. But, typically Filipina, they were so feminine and pretty. And so shy as to be timid.

"Our Lola is preparing an octopus for your supper," I answered.

"We're having octopus tonight, Lola?" another of the girls asked.

"Soon," our Lola replied. "It is boiling now with the rice. I will have to chop it up first."

Another of the girls looked at the small stove near the kitchen door where I was preparing my meal. "What is that, *Tito* Mississippi?" she asked. "You're making another mess. Why do you have a cloth and crushed soybeans?"

"Tito" means uncle and is used as a term of endearment, like "Lola" is. Sometimes, I assume according to their mood, they called me *kuya*, which means sibling or cousin.

"I make tofu," I answered. "With instructions from my Peace Corps manual."

"Why don't you buy tofu at the marketplace?" another of the girls asked.

"Because I want to know how to make it. I can buy in America."

"And you can buy it here. So, what is the difference?"

"Because it comes from here," I replied.

"It comes from China," they all answered me in unison.

"It's the same thing."

"You are so weird, Tito Mississippi," one girl said, laughing while shaking her head.

"When does Tita Lois come again?" another girl asked.

"This weekend," I answered.

"She needs to show us again how to do the dance from Egypt," the girl said. "I want to demonstrate it in one of my classes."

"You and Tita Lois are so quiet when you are in your room," the first girl noted. "What do you do up there? Aren't you afraid of scandal?"

"Americans don't know scandal," I teased.

"Americans are shameless," they all said.

"Why do you stay up there all alone when she is gone?" one of the girls asked.

"She is your *kasama*," another said. "Aren't you lonely with her gone?"

"Of course," I replied.

"Why do you stay all by yourself in your room then, if you are lonely?"

69

"Because you have bad breath," I answered back with a forced straight face.

"You are always joking, Tito Mississippi," she answered back.

"I have so many things I want to do," I replied.

"Like play your guitar," one said. "Why don't you play for us more often?"

"You are always studying," I replied. "Besides, I like to read and play the radio. I just have so much to do upstairs. I don't need a *kasama*. Thank you, though."

I felt restless later on as I sat in my room. But now there were these blatant and open feelings for Lois, which changed my outlook about everything and in the process changed my daily routine. I still liked to read, or play guitar, or listen to the radio. But sometimes I just wanted her and spent time doing nothing but daydreaming about her. Why was she so special? Maybe she wasn't. Maybe it was just being half way around the world, plus the culture shock, that caused all this ache inside me. But all that made her specialness more appealing, for I determined she was indeed special.

She was pretty, but that wasn't it. She held herself with dignity and reserve. That was part of it. She seemed such a good person. I loved her for that. She wanted things, but not only ambitious things.

I was not the most religious Jew in the world, but on the other hand, I was proud of my heritage. The Jews separated themselves from what they determined the pagan world. I had this long heritage inside me. While I wanted happiness and prosperity, I also wanted to stand out as special, too. To be up to changing the world in some way, big or small, for the better.

I saw the same thing in Lois.

The way she wanted to help people in her village. Not just by being a teacher, but by getting involved in the water project, for instance. That might sound like a typical Peace Corps objective, but I knew a lot of PCVs who couldn't find anything to do. She tutored her two top students at night. They weren't just smart; she saw a spark in them and knew she could give them confidence and direction, as well as a way out, out of horrific squalor. I admired her for that. But there was more. I cared like that too. Seeing it in her made it feel like a personal favor to me somehow. So she was indeed special in my eyes.

Now that we were officially an us, of sorts, she was part of my routine in addition to coming home for a cold beer, a small workout, cooking supper, then reading, or music. And now something always reminded me of her. Maybe it was something I wanted to share with her or tell her. Or sometimes I just wanted to feel her presence.

After finishing a book I had been reading the last few days, I was still bored. I felt listless and didn't want to start another. I turned on my radio that doubled as a cassette player. It was always tuned into Radio Mindanao. At this time in the early evening, Muslim songs played. A man, something like a disc jockey perhaps, talked in a harsh, screeching voice. I had no idea what the DJ was saying, but it intrigued me. The dialect wasn't Tagalog, nor anything similar, that I could tell. Someone explained to me he talked in *Iranon*, a Muslim dialect native to the coastal area in Mindanao where most Muslims lived. To listen to the DJ made me feel a castaway, as if wandering off in a ship or exploring unknown waters, hoping I didn't fall off the edge of the world as I did so. This mood, at least, got me out of my boredom.

The music was exotic. Usually a simple guitar was the only accompaniment. Chords played in tune with the song, but the commotion on the guitar seemed more like a drum the way it was pounded on. One song had the singer blaring out words, in Iranon, to the melody of "Oh My Darling, Clementine." The worst part was I liked it and longed to know what it said.

But there was a song that knocked me down, the melody hypnotic. Was the song about mundane life in Mindanao or was it about the Quran or perhaps Muhammad? But it carried no rephrase or chorus. And it needed one. As much as I liked the melody, the singer sang one verse after another, perhaps four or five verses in all.

I grabbed my guitar from the chair next to where I sat and searched for the chord. A-minor. I loved that progression. When the song completed, I hummed out the melody as I strummed the guitar trying to learn all the chord requirements. I found them. I continued to hum the melody until I got enough feel of it to derive a rephrase melody. I found one. That excited me. What if I found the author and gave this rephrase melody to him, I pondered. But I knew he wouldn't want an American chromosome in his song, especially that of a Jew. Such is the world, I decided.

And why wasn't Lois here to share this? Surely no other Peace Corps Volunteer thought things like I just did. Or so I liked believing. And I was sure Lois would be all the more taken by me because of it, which made me long for her all the more.

Chapter 8

Mt. Carmel was a Southern Baptist missionary group. They were just off the main highway to Digos, approximately three-fourths of the way there from Cotabato City. This meant Lois and I could take a regular, full-sized bus. In good faith we brought supplies and the beehive for Margaret. We had to get it to her even if we didn't get treated to a free transport by our missionary friends. Mt. Carmel was on the lower edge of Mt. Apo, even on her side of the mountain. Convenient for us either way.

Once we arrived at the provincial capital, we prepared to board a jeepney for the last leg up to the mission itself.

"Mississippi," someone from a van called out exuberantly. There were several Filipinos in the van with the man who called out to me. All were looking in my direction.

"The driver is the one from Tennessee," Lois said.

"They're all from Tennessee," I replied.

"One's from Alabama," she corrected, "and there's one from Kentucky."

"Hey," I replied to the driver, not remembering anyone's name.

"Were you coming to see us?" the driver asked.

"That's exactly where we were headed," I answered. "Do you have room for us?"

"We'll find room for Mississippi," he said with a laugh. "You'll have to leave the Yankee behind, though," he said with a wink. "Just joshing with you, ma'am. We're always happy to see someone from home."

I pulled our backpacks and bee supplies off the jeepney we had prepared to board.

"Is all that yours?" the van's driver asked as he came to help us load. "It might be a squeeze. Where you headed with that?"

"That's what I was coming to talk to y'all about," I explained. "I was hoping you could get us to Mt. Apo. Not the top of it, though."

He thought for a moment as he raised the back door, exposing the luggage area.

"Let me talk it over with Reverend," he said in his Southern drawl, "but I'm sure we can help you out. These good folk in the van, here, came to us from Cebu. There's a mission near there, and we exchange personnel and resources sometimes. Let me get them settled, if you don't mind, and we'll see what the Reverend says."

He had to unpack most of the luggage area to get the beehive box in securely. Lois and I kept our backpacks with us, because the hive and bagged supplies barely found space with all the luggage for the people from Cebu.

"You're Lois, aren't you?" the driver asked us as he drove toward the mission.

"Why, yes, I am," she said, showing approval of his memory.

"I remember you because you're the only Quaker I ever met."

"Is that good?" she asked.

"We serve the same Master," he said.

"That we do," she replied. She then turned toward me and mouthed, *and what about you*? Meaning me.

I nodded facetiously, feeling rather like a childish cut-up.

"Do y'all like your sites?" the driver asked further, momentarily turning his head back toward Lois and me. We were riding in the back seat. "We see Mississippi here every once in a while, but what about you, Lois? Is it what you expected?"

"It's never quite what you expect," she answered, "but it's in the realm, I suppose. I'm happy. Feeling productive."

"That's good. And you, Mississippi? You were starting beehives before. And training bank personnel on the computer. You held some classes in household bookkeeping. What else you got going? Besides that beehive you're ready to install, which speaks for itself."

"That's about it," I answered. "I get involved in some cottage industry, too, but nothing ever comes from it. But a couple of months ago, when I was at my bi-monthly Central Bank meeting in Manila, I saw a presentation about the worst rat infestation in the Philippines. In Midsayap, on the island of Mindanao. I couldn't believe it. That's just up the road from Cotabato City. An hour away on the national highway, in fact."

"That area has great farm land," the driver said. "Maybe that's it. They have some plush, well-irrigated rice land there. I guess the rats thrive."

"Anyway," I continued, "as soon as I got back from Manila I went there. I met with the Agricultural office and with the Rotary Club there. They have a couple of universities there, too. I went to the mayor's office and arranged a town meeting. We got sponsors and bought rat poison and killed twenty thousand rats. We cut off the tail of each dead rat and bundled them by fifties. Twenty thousand fewer vermin there now in Midsayap. Ha."

"You do good work, Mississippi," the driver complimented. "There's a lot of good Peace Corps Volunteers, but you really get involved. You would have made a good missionary. Too bad you're not Baptist."

"I'll settle to be a chosen," I said, smiling.

"God's chosen." He returned the smile. "That you are."

Lois grabbed my hand and squeezed it in celebration.

"So, how are you doing with those bees, then?" he asked. "Is anyone making money off of them?"

"Not yet," I replied. "We haven't really gotten that far. You really need two hives, at least, so you have enough honey and bees and all. I only have one hive each in two places, and will have only one where I'm going. I'm just trying to get things going and see if it kicks in, and I'll try to expand to two hives from the one eventually. I'd have to get a second queen for that, of course, but I want to see if the first hive expands well and we can split it. But I'm just not having luck. It's more than luck, actually. I'm not getting response. There's some real good farmers, but with all these starving, destitute farmers I work with, I thought I'd find more that wanted to improve their lot. One of my new hives is with a rich accountant. I didn't come here to make the rich richer, but if this guy is interested and puts forth the effort, it still helps Filipinos, and even the small farmers will benefit from the pollination."

"That's just human nature," the driver explained. "Everywhere you go it's like that. Some places more than others, but it's a human trait. There's limited resources in the world, Mississippi, and you have to pick your winners. When this mission was opened, we were interested in saving souls for the Lord. We still are. But we learned when someone is struggling—and it's often more than struggling here, so many are fighting to stay alive—we found they weren't much listening to us about their souls. It's already a religious country. They didn't need any more preaching or liturgies. They needed a full belly, a roof over their head, and someone to show them kindness. Well, if you love the Lord, you do want to work to enrich their souls, but we found it better to start by enriching their lives. Jesus fed the five thousand. With His help we'll feed who we can. But our resources are limited, and we have to start with those that respond to us, and even then the most competent. Those who can learn from us and pass it on to the rest of their community. So, I hear what you're saying, Mississippi, but it becomes a science and an art how to get it done."

"That's for sure," I seconded.

"Some of the people we work with," he continued, "are so destitute, and the malnutrition so severe, we have to find a way to improve things at all. There are some local berries from bushes we grow, they grow wild, but of course we enhance their growth, and we make snow cones out of the juice and give it to them. It's rich in vitamin C. And there is just no protein available for the worst off of these people. But just giving them food is a dead-end street. Some of that is okay in the short run, and at times resources need to be spared for some in the short run. But what happens when we leave? Plus, it makes them dependent. We gave a village leader an Anglo-Nubian goat once. These are big goats, much bigger than the native goat. They produce a good bit of milk. If you start giving the milk to young Filipino children, they develop the ability to digest it. So, we gave the village leader one of our nanny goats, hoping he would breed it with a native goat and produce a herd for milk. Instead, on the very first weekend, he slaughtered the goat and had a barrio fiesta. It was more for status than to feed his friends, too. It really is a science, Mississippi. Even an art, like I said. How to do any good. The desperation is so overwhelming, and resources must be used to turn it around somehow. So don't get disheartened. You're doing a great job."

When we arrived at the mission, Lois and I waited as the others unpacked and found their way. Lois and I walked around to reminisce from previous visits. Happily, it was approved that we could go further in the mission van. All the way to Margaret's.

"You mean to say you walked all the way here the last time you visited her?" Lois asked, marveling, as we stopped in front of the Nipa Hut that was Margaret's.

"It beats waiting on a jeepney," I said.

"You'd have been in a fix had I not brought you this time," the mission driver commented. "I clocked twelve miles since we turned off the main road. Twelve miles uphill. The incline surely was thirty degrees."

"You always walk this?" Lois asked, still

seemingly agape at the idea.

"I've only been here twice," I said.

"That's forty-eight miles in all," the driver said.

I nodded, wallowing in the heroics made of my endeavors.

Margaret appeared by the time we got the van unloaded.

"Where did you just come from?" I asked her. "I brought your bee supplies. And listen, I was given free a hive box for you. And I have instructions on how to make two different kinds of hive boxes so that you don't have to depend on me. I have three slats of worker bees, too, and wax foundations for twenty more. You'll need these. There's a ridge on these wax foundations for every honeycomb cell. If we leave it to the bees, for some reason I've had problems with them making the cells too big. That ends up producing drones. Drones don't work, or fight, they just fertilize the eggs."

Margaret's eyes lit up as she scoped out all the things I brought her.

"Look at you, Mississippi!" She gleamed my way. "Wow, I hit the jackpot today. Where did I come from just now, you asked? I just came from my vegetable garden. I created a small terraced garden like your mission showed us for SALT," Margaret explained turning toward the driver. Then she looked at Lois and me and explained, "SALT stands for sloped agricultural land technology, in case you two have forgotten. That's where I was when I saw you drive up. In my SALT garden."

"Good for you, Margaret," the driver praised. "Good for you that you're using SALT. That's exactly what we need. Learn the local skills needed, and spread the knowledge, and set an example as you do. That'll make everyone at the mission happy. That's why we like working with the Peace Corps."

"Isn't a drone a male bee?" Margaret asked. "Back to the subject at hand. Maybe it was your queen's idea to create so many drones," Margaret said with a grin, "where that so-called problem occurred. She obviously likes her eggs fertilized, catch my drift."

"Whatever," I said, managing a chuckle for the fun of it. "I brought you glue, hammer, nails, wood, a level. I don't know what you have. You just get started, and next time I see you, let me know what else you need."

"I really appreciate this," Margaret said. "You do more for me than any agency around. Not complaining, but it's nice to have Peace Corps around me. They understand better what another PCV needs. All the Filipinos think we're with the CIA anyway."

"You're joking," the driver said with a laugh.

"I wish she was," Lois said. "Who gives up America and a career to come here and live like this? No one, they decide, so we must all be CIA, not PCVs. That's the way the locals see it."

"Missionaries give up all the luxuries of America to come here," the driver said.

"But you're religious, and it's a career of sorts," I added. "We barely get paid. Somehow it just doesn't compute with Filipinos. Actually, I prefer being considered CIA rather than lazy or not ready to find a job. That's what people back home lay on you if you make a career of the military. You can't win. If you serve, if you mean it—ha, you're worthless. Better to be a spy for the evil Central Intelligence Agency of

America."

"I suppose." Margaret sighed. "I took a sabbatical as a college professor to do this. I resent being considered a spy, myself. I came to help, to learn, and to teach. 'If you don't appreciate it, it's your problem' is how I feel about it."

"So, do you have everything you need?" the driver asked as he closed the back of the van.

"We're set," I replied.

He stuck out his hand, and we all bid him farewell.

"So, what brings you here, Lois?" Margaret asked. "What a pleasant surprise."

"I knew Mississippi needed help with all this," Lois answered. "He brought some things for me, too, and it's my way of paying him back."

"Well, I'm happy to have you here. It's nice to have company. Rhonda and Jennifer make it up here occasionally. Sometimes we meet in town, in the provincial capital, usually—it's the most convenient place to meet between the three of us. But sometimes we go to Davao. We'd all go crazy if we didn't get away now and then."

"I know what you mean," Lois said sympathetically. "Mississippi gets to visit us at our sites, but also, he goes around his province with his bank. Then he gets expenses paid to and from Manila every two months, put up by the Central Bank. So, the rest of us need what we can get now and then."

"How's the little goat?" I asked Margaret, to change the subject.

"He died three days after you brought him here," Margaret replied. "I don't know what that rash was, but he didn't make it. I gave him milk, leaves, and water.

He seemed to be recovering, but didn't. More death in the Philippines." Margaret looked at Lois for emphasis. "Mississippi carried that sick goat up this incline for eight of the twelve-mile walk, Lois. He found him abandoned in one of the villages toward the base of the mountain. Isn't he a champion? And the goat died anyway."

"Speaking of death," Lois broke in, "you heard about the mayor, right?"

"Of Zamboanga?" Margaret asked sadly.

Lois and I nodded yes.

"Is there going to be a revolution?" Margaret shook her head. "Come on inside," she said leading the way to her Nipa Hut. "We'll have coffee while we talk. There's so much to talk about these days. We still have a year to go here. Are we going to be allowed to stay? When me and the girls go to Davao, there's security check points on the highway. The NPA seems more a threat every day. I understand why. I'm not advocating a revolution, and I'm no advocate of Chairman Mao's little red book. But I understand why people are angry and why, in that anger, communism seems a solution."

She studied me to see my reaction.

"I'm no commie pinko, Mississippi, hear me out," she continued. "Even though I'm a liberal from Massachusetts, and a feminist. I'm just saying I understand how it looks to these people in their rice paddies, with nothing, and no future, because of a despotic puppet of American policy."

"Actually, me too, Margaret," I said to the surprise of both her and Lois. "I'm more of a capitalist than I ever was, as far as economic policy is concerned, and I still believe in all I did when I joined the Marines trying to go to Vietnam. It wasn't open and shut for me then, and it sure is complex here. But I agree. What is the guy in the rice paddy supposed to think? He can't see that a communist tyranny is going to be even worse than Marcos. He's desperate for anything different. And different to him means better than status quo somehow. He feels radicalized enough to want something better, even if it turns out worse. Until he's stuck with that worse. I hope it comes to some kind of a head soon. I want answers this time. This time I did get sent to Vietnam, so to speak, and I am fighting for freedom in my own way now, too. But it's so complicated."

"And the MNLF is right there where Mississippi lives," Lois added. "The Muslims are a proud people anyway, and lost a civil war. They're just as angry. It's ugly everywhere you go."

Margaret led us up the bamboo ladder into her one-room hut. It was built and laid out much like Lois'.

"You at least have running water available," Lois admired. "And the air is so nice here. So cool and crisp. It feels marvelous to get out of the muggy heat."

"Running water?" Margaret groaned. "Pray tell, girl, what do you mean?"

"Your sink here," Lois said pointing. "You have a hand pump in it."

"So, what do you do?" Margaret inquired.

"Walk a mile carrying plastic containers," Lois replied.

"My Lord, how do you manage? I thought I had it rough. Or inconvenient. I almost prefer being twelve miles from town to what you're going through."

"So, how do you manage?" Lois asked, sharing hardship stories. "You don't have access to anything."

"I have a nice vegetable garden. I'll show it to you. But I do depend on town for everything else. It's not so bad, really. A jeepney comes by once in the morning. Then the same jeepney goes back down in the afternoon. You passed through a couple of little villages—if that's the word—on your way here, and there's another one a couple of miles up the road. Then there's the forestry office nearby. They're always checking up on me. For security reasons, too. There's enough need that we have jeepney service. Sometimes I get stuck in town when I go in. I could walk up the incline like Mississippi here, but I usually find a lodge for the night. And feel like I'm on vacation. So don't pity me."

Margaret drew water from her hand pump, got out some coffee beans, put them in a hand grinder, and processed them into a brew of coffee. "Listen," she explained as she did so, "I only have this one hammock. Rhonda and Jennifer sleep on the floor. I have a large mat that you'll have to share, if you don't mind."

"We don't mind," Lois returned.

Margaret looked at us and grinned. "Somehow I had the feeling you wouldn't." Lois blushed. I tried to hold back a smirk, but couldn't. "Should I regret not having a spare room for you two?"

"Regret the hell out of it, Margaret," I joked.

"I knew it," Margaret teased right back. "So, when did this happen? I knew there was more to it than poor Mississippi, our resident ex-Marine, needing help from a sweet little Quaker girl. I saw it coming in Zambo. Even San Diego. Everyone did, except you two. Tell me all the disgusting details. This is better than the TV I don't have."

"Nothing to tell," Lois said. She looked at me menacingly as if to tell me I should watch my mouth. "Nothing at all. Got it?"

My smirk broadened.

"There isn't much to tell, Margaret," I explained. "The angels did start singing, but we live far enough away from each other, and we have to do our jobs. But then again, we live close enough to each other, and there is desire inside." I stared Lois down. I was going to speak my mind on this matter. "There is desire. But in this setting, we have to have discipline."

"Desire, you say?" Margaret quizzed. "Not just flirtation?"

"Absolutely," Lois and I said in unison. "Deep feelings," Lois emphasized.

Margaret nodded at us with a look a mother would give. "I wish you both the best. Were something to come of this, all of us on Mindanao want to be a part. Especially me, Rhonda, and Jenny. You will hurt us if you leave us out. Do you catch my drift?"

Lois answered by a hand salute while straightening to attention.

"So, me and the other girls," Margaret said, "are going to Davao tomorrow. You met those guys in the PCV group ahead of us before. The ones that live in Davao. The waterboys. We're all going to meet at their house and tie one on."

"You make it sound like an orgy," Lois said with a grin.

"Well, I'm too old and too feminist to even contemplate something like that. I don't know about Rhonda and Jenn, but they've never indulged yet, to my knowledge. But you know what I mean. If you didn't have Mississippi here to unwind around, you'd go bananas. Come with us. We just want to have a few San Miguels, eat some *chicherone*, and some *kinilaw*."

"I'm not into pork or raw fish," I said.

"You're kosher?" Margaret asked.

I nodded that I was. "Not fully, since there's no rabbi around to prepare kosher meats. Technically, because there's no *shochet*, that's the rabbi that handles all the preparations, everything is *treif*. But I still don't break the ban on pork and blood and such. I'm not super strict or I'd go vegetarian."

"Who cares?" Margaret harped. "You like San Miguel. Eat what you want. We need a break. It's great the two of you are here. It'll feel like a party. I need a party."

"What if we had come tomorrow?" Lois asked. "With all of this stuff. You wouldn't have been here."

"I know to leave it with the Ministry of Agriculture," I explained. "They're next door. They'd keep it for her."

"I want to dance when we get to Davao," Lois said. "I haven't danced since Zambo. Do you dance when you go out in Davao?"

"There's a place we all go," Margaret assured. "Speaking of orgies, it's at a brothel. And none of us indulge there, just dance. Maybe the waterboys do when we're not there. But even if they do, they're polite enough to wait until we leave. The dancing is wild there, and the drinks strong and abundant."

"Just my style," Lois said in glee.

It was the checkpoints that intimidated the girls along the way to Davao the next day. I had been through a few in Mindanao at times, but thought little of it. Seeing the revulsion and concern of the PCV women I rode the bus with, I began to wonder why those stops barely caught my attention before.

I had been through checkpoints in Communist Bulgaria. They checked my passport at every stop, in fact. I was in Iran two months before the Shah fell and the warning went out against Americans. I rode a bus through the Khyber Pass from Communist-held Afghanistan into Pakistan. I was in the Marines, in Okinawa, the day it reverted from American control back to Japan. I was issued my gas mask, rifle, and bayonet because of a Red Guard threat. I saw the aftermath of a terrorist attack on an Israeli highway. Somehow these little checkpoints in Mindanao seemed routine. Almost harmless. But the girls saw it differently.

"Those reptilian eyes." Margaret scowled at the guards at the checkpoint, leaning toward us, almost whispering. "I hear they're trained to just take people out."

"The elite forces are trained to do that," Rhonda concurred. "I heard they're trained by our own Special Forces troops."

"They might be trained by our guys," I commented, "but that doesn't mean they're trained to just shoot any old civilian."

The girls looked at me for a moment and then re-centered their attention on the checkpoints. I was showing my redneck to them again, somehow, I decided.

"Did you catch how cold and distant these soldiers appear when they scope you out?" Jennifer sneered. "No sign of life at all in them. Like some robot from

Star Wars. Who's a threat, who isn't?"

"They're doing their job." I intervened yet again. This reminded me of my Vietnam era days. The military was the most guilty in the history of guilt as far as so many people thought. "There are suicide personnel coming at them, and there are groups of terrorists trying to make it through. Some with weapons. These guys are trying to do their jobs and stay alive too. They can't fight off many threats. They're stuck out in the middle of nowhere in the dead of night and are easily sitting ducks. And it's their ass if some offender gets through."

The girls stared at me again, but I didn't care. I was no fan of the Marcos regime, and I even had sympathy with why some people didn't want to keep things the way they were, but this was just paranoia to me, the way these girls talked. They didn't know anything, and I was tired of being the bad guy. Still, I was aware I didn't know enough of how things worked inside the Marcos military to take up for anybody very much. I was trying to pacify old wounds inside me more than anything.

Before the conversation could continue, the bus slowed to a stop. I saw Filipinos standing up to look out the front and sides of the bus near the driver. Suddenly, the bus doors opened and a military guard boarded. He said something in Tagalog and the passengers began to pick up their belongings and exit the bus.

"We're being told to disembark from the bus," Lois explained to us. "Up ahead, a jeepney has been hit by NPA guerillas. The highway is blocked. Another bus is coming to take us the rest of the way."

"Was that Tagalog?" Jennifer asked Lois. "In my

village it's mostly *Illacano,* the dialect in northern Luzon where Marcos is from. I barely understood anything the guard said at all."

"We speak *Cebuano*," Rhonda said.

"*Illongo*," Margaret said. "Not that I know any."

We walked by the mutilated jeepney and did our best not to look at the dead bodies strewn outside on the highway and areas adjacent to it. As much as we wanted to see the extent of the attack, we were scared to look. Not just at the death and destruction all around us, but to not look more conspicuous than we already were as white-skinned Americans.

As we approached the bus waiting on us to continue our journey, armed guards inspected each and every one of us. Reptilian stares were again directed our way, guns pointed at our heads, as well as at the other passengers. Each and every one of us was frisked before we were released to board.

"I hope they never make a ride out of this at Disney World," Margaret scoffed from our new seats as she lit up a cigarette.

I shook my head in frustration as I thought about what we'd just experienced.

"In Zambo and where I'm at," I said, "they made a peace treaty with the Moslems. There's still danger, but here there is open warfare with the NPA. Not even the pretense of a peace treaty."

We had gone a few miles and were just minutes short of our destination in Davao when we heard a grinding noise behind us on the highway. Instantly, we jerked in our seats to see what it was. It sounded ominous. Five armored vehicles raced by our bus as we pulled over to let them pass. On top of each were six soldiers pointing machine guns in different directions, front and back. One on each corner of the tank and two in the middle. No one made a comment. What lay ahead of us? Was this to be a new version of PCV R&R?

We wanted to do nothing that night except relax when we finally arrived at the house where the PCV waterboys lived. At first we weren't in the mood to talk about any of our adventures, due to depression and complete emotional exhaustion. As the waterboys pestered us, however, we couldn't talk fast enough. I soon tired of it, though, and went to sleep on the straw mat on the floor near a bed that we reserved for Margaret. These new memories needed to find their way to reconcile with my old ones from previous years, and sleep was the cure for that.

Somewhere during the night I felt Lois lie down next to me. How I got so tired I'll never know, but in spite of crashing early, I was also the last one up. And even then it was because Lois was bent over me, one hand on my chest, one stroking my cheek, as if worried about her little boy.

"The girls and I need to go shopping," she said. "We need you to come with us. We need a male chaperone. There are military patrols around. Something's going on, but the girls and I need to shop. So many of our clothes have been worn out from hand washings by coconut shells and stones. Come, darling mine. I'm even out of underwear, and my last bra is about finished, also. The girls know Davao and told me about an American kind of store here, the only one in all of Mindanao that has American clothing. It's the only store that has a bra big enough for me. Surely, that should get your energy flowing again. Can you manage? We need you, sweets."

I lay there silently a bit longer. Were my brain parts still processing? I couldn't possibly be this tired, but I was. Finally, I opened my eyes and managed a half smile her way. I hated shopping, but I loved being needed.

To get a jump on the day, we decided to eat brunch during our shopping excursion. But it was all for naught. A jeepney on the street in front of our house was turned away by a military barricade that was forming. What now?

"What's this about?" Lois asked one of the waterboys from the edge of their yard.

He shook his head and shrugged that he didn't know. More military was coming our way. Then more. They were headed right for the house where we were staying. We almost wondered if they were coming to get us. Or perhaps to protect us. We knew that couldn't be the case, but no better answers came in the confusion.

"I see what's happening," another of the waterboys said.

Before he could explain, we all understood. Right in front of us, what looked to be thousands of protestors approached from the nearby highway. They came in droves of vehicles, disembarked, and, for whatever reason, the very house where we were staying with our PCV Davao-located friends became the center point of a massive protest. What they were protesting we hadn't a clue.

"That's what we get for renting a house near the highway on the edge of town," a waterboy said.

"How were we supposed to know?" one of his

roommates whined. "This house is near the Water District offices, and it's easy to do our projects in the farms nearby."

"My God, they're still swarming in," Margaret said, gawking.

As the military, both troops and tanks, approached to confront the protestors, it was our house that was the battle line. Soon, without explanation or apology, the military contingent took over the yard where we stood watching. As the crowd of protestors got larger, missile launchers were brought, in addition to more troops and tanks being positioned in front of and near our house grounds, some right in our very yard.

"For God's sake," one of the waterboys exclaimed, "those two tanks are headed right for our house. Are they going to knock it down? My stuff's in there. My personal stuff. Not just my possessions, but sentimental items. Damn this."

The protestors kept coming also. Lines and lines of them. As they approached the soldiers themselves, some of them began climbing the shoulders of other protestors at the front, as if to block the military from going any further.

We were now being hurried back into the house by the soldiers. It was encouraging in that maybe they weren't intending to demolish the house as we feared, but we still couldn't be sure that commotion and gunfire wouldn't damage the house and our goods inside. And perhaps us, too.

"I'm going shopping," Lois said angrily.

"You're crazy," one of the waterboys said.

"It might be safer at the store," Jennifer suggested.

"I'm not leaving my things," another of the

waterboys said angrily.

"I'm going shopping," Lois repeated in an even more determined tone of voice. "Everyone but the Davao PCVs needs to get out of here. Bring along whatever you hold valuable, just in case the worst happens, but we need to leave. And actually, I don't care who goes or stays. This is my day to be a normal person again, and no one, absolutely no one, is going to deny me." She looked at me. "Come, Mississippi. Let's go."

It felt like an order, but I had no problem with it.

"How you going to get out of here?" one of the waterboys asked.

"Somehow," Lois replied.

"You're starting to sound like Mississippi," Margaret said with a grin. "Bahala na it is, then. The great whatever prevails. I'm game."

Lois, myself, and the girls made for the back yard. By now it also was full of military troops, but as yet no protestors.

"There's the chief officer," Lois said, pointing at an indignant, well-dressed officer at the front of the troops. "Look at all those ribbons and the fancy designs on his head cover. He's got to be the guy in charge."

As the rest of us inspected him to see if we agreed with her assessment, Lois walked straight toward him and pushed her way through those soldiers surrounding him. One of the soldiers readied a pistol, but the officer of our intentions waved his hand to tell the guy it was okay.

Lois said something in Tagalog to the officer. Whatever it was seemed to work. He held out his elbow for her to cling to, motioned for the girls and myself to follow, and then walked us through the impasse and out into the street until we reached an area resembling normalcy. He waved down a jeepney for us and talked to the driver. Within minutes, we were at the store of our dreams. Lois could not erase her smirk of joy— until we got inside. Then her preoccupation with reality, meaning shopping, returned.

That afternoon we decided it might be safe to return to the house. When we arrived back, except for tank tracks in the yard and debris strewn everywhere, things looked sane again.

"What happened after we left?" Margaret asked the boys.

"It broke up just a few minutes after you left," one of them answered. "I still don't know what it was about, but there was no violence, and very little confrontation except for what you witnessed. I hope you got your shopping done. I'm ready to tie one on. Let's get ready to boogie."

It's ironic that the freest any of us felt our entire time in the Philippines was that night at the brothel. I wasn't going to condemn any PCV brethren for partaking at such a place. If it had not been for my relationship with Lois, I could imagine I might feel a need to unwind in such a way myself. What the waterboys did on their own time I didn't know. This night was for dancing. Our PCV girls kept calling it ferocious dancing. A seeming desperation to unwind. To get out the bad spiritual air and breathe in something better. Poetically speaking, of course.

"Here's what we do," one of the waterboys explained. "Mississippi and the rest of us guys are going to buy Cokes for the prostitutes over there. This will pay our way for being here. You're our dates, so let us be macho guys and pay your way by buying these ladies of the night their Cokes and making them feel they earned their keep. Dance with us, or with each other, or by yourself. Just unwind. This is your night on the town."

He looked each of us straight in the eyes one at a time to make sure we understood the agenda. Then he said further, "And welcome to Davao."

Chapter 9

I was getting to know more of the farmers with every monthly Samahang Nayon meeting. Though I still seldom knew what was being discussed, I enjoyed finding out, from the farmers themselves, their conditions and attitudes. These meetings were the most convenient way to accomplish this. Since I was just passing through, so to speak, I enjoyed talking more from a curious level than a professional one. It helped me gain perspective on what our bank could do to help them.

I talked Lois into attending a meeting with me. It was one of two cooperatives near her village. She had never been to a Samahang Nayon meeting before and wanted to see one. But I needed her for translations at times, too, with some of the farmers.

It was a Friday afternoon, and she made arrangements to come in with me and our bank team back to Cotabato City afterwards. This required a jeepney ride from the Samahang Nayon, the short way to the coconut tree trunk bridge we all had to take. But for once, she now had a ride in the bank jeep waiting on us at the other side of the small river, all the way to Cotabato City.

Word was out about my singing. I now opened every single monthly meeting at every single Samahang Nayon with a song. Attendance was up because everyone knew this American guy, me, was going to be there and sing. I now, as a matter of course, brought my own guitar, a cheap but functional one I'd found in a shop in town.

And finally, to my glee, Lois was there to behold me doing my musical thing.

After the meeting, we sat next to the Samahang Nayon president as we ate. He was one of the more responsive and successful of those I worked with on projects. His yield increased significantly from the fertilizer machine I brought for him from the International Rice Research Institute, the one Lois had helped me cart from the airport. The IRRI agent who introduced the machine to me was so pleased with this farmer that he flew all the way from Manila to hand deliver a machine made especially to share with the rest of his Samahang Nayon, with the stipulation that the president show other farmers in his cooperative how to use it. The president of this Samahang Nayon also expanded his backyard fish ponds to two. Each was twenty yards in length and ten yards in width. It supplemented his diet well, and he even sold surplus in the local market place.

"How many acres do you own?" I asked him.

"I own what in America would be twenty acres," he answered. "With irrigation, I harvest three times a year. Even in the dry season I get good harvests."

I looked around. His farm was where we held our meetings for this group. "You have pigs and ducks, too," I mentioned.

"And chickens," he replied. "I even have surplus eggs for the market. I also sell *balut* on the market."

"What is *balut*?" Lois asked.

I looked at her and made a face. "You don't want to know."

The Samahang Nayon president laughed. "It is duck fetus," he said.

"It's a developing embryo," I explained further. "Fertilized duck eggs hatch in about three weeks. The buyers wait until a couple of days before the egg hatches and then boil it in water. Then they add soy sauce or whatever spices."

"I am sorry I asked," Lois said, squirming. She looked at me directly. "Have you ever eaten one?" she asked me.

"It's not kosher," I answered.

"You little cop-out." She laughed. "You get to weasel out of every inconvenience with some obscure Jewish law somewhere. And how is it not kosher?" she challenged. "You can eat eggs. You can eat chicken. And duck."

"We don't eat blood," I replied, grinning over my gotcha. "But I'd dream something up if I had to. I thought about eating it once. Just to see. I didn't get past the smell. Then the Filipino I was with cracked his open, and I saw this shriveled up duck fetus. Gross. But one night I was on a bus to Manila during my week for Central Bank meetings. Coming in from the countryside somewhere. It was pitch dark, and the roadside vendor was selling food items. Including balut. I made up my mind I was going to really do it this time. Eat it in the dark and not look at it. I cracked the shell open. *Whoof!* The smell got to me. But I gutted it out. I psyched myself up and put it up to my mouth. And just as I was ready to take a bite, here comes a bus with its lights from the opposite direction, and there was this duck fetus staring right at me. I couldn't do it. I gave it to a little girl in the seat behind me."

Lois laughed in mock victory. "So much for the Marines," she said.

I let her enjoy herself a bit before turning back to the Samahang Nayon president.

"How many are there like you in this Samahang Nayon?" I asked him. "You have twenty acres. Do any other farmers have as much or bigger?"

"One farmer has fifteen acres. Two have ten. Three have eight acres. Most are five acres or less. Several only own two acres."

"We don't get our loans paid off by many in your group," I said.

"They don't have much left after they pay back the Chinese traders," he answered. "If the traders don't get their money back, they bring men to collect. Our bank has American money. The farmers know this. They look at the bank loan as aid. Or at least many do. The smallest farmers, the ones with less than five acres, they have a bit of fruit for a meal besides rice. If they are lucky, they catch a catfish in a stream now and then. Occasionally they kill a chicken they own. Their one normal full meal is of rice with a pinch of salt. They call it spot. A spot of salt. They never have enough to pay a loan."

"I guess Mr. Rancon knows this," I said. "The bank even has me trying to collect loans. I don't really collect, I explain our problem to some that don't pay back these delinquent loans. I hope the Peace Corps doesn't find out I'm doing this. But the bank leaves me only the bigger farmers and some of the businessmen that borrow. I went to one house to collect, and it was a two-story house, very nicely furnished, with new paint. The bank is just a sucker. That's what people think."

The president nodded agreement.

"James and Lois," the president said suddenly, as if surprised about something. "I notice you only have well water to drink. Aren't you afraid to get sick? Our well is safe from amoeba, but we did not think to boil it for you to protect from germs."

"We're okay," Lois assured. "We're acclimated now."

"But it's the tropics," the president fretted, "and every area is different from the others." He looked around frantically until he spotted his son. "*Anak*," he called out. "*Tuba.*" The president then pointed up toward the top of a coconut tree.

"*Anak* means child," Lois translated.

"I know," I replied. "I know that from a Freddie Aguilar song. But the president here said *tuba*, too, and that's coconut wine. I hate that stuff."

"Not kosher?" Lois chided me. "How have you survived that anti-social aspect in your obliged cultural interchange?"

"It's kosher, but they don't know it."

I looked frantically at the president, hoping to stop his kid from climbing the coconut tree at the edge of the yard before it was too late.

"No tuba," I yelped.

The president looked at me to make sure he heard correctly. He then turned back to his son, who was already at the base of the coconut tree, ready to make his ascent. The president then shouted out a string of instructions to his son, who left the group of coconut trees in front of him for another group in another area of the yard.

"Watch how he all but runs up that coconut tree," I said to Lois. "It should be an Olympic sport."

The boy jumped as high up on the trunk of the tree as he could. Then, like a bear running vertically with arms and legs synced left and right, he shimmied barefoot to the ripe coconuts just under the palm-like branches at the top. Holding on with one hand and gripping the tree trunk with his knees, the boy took a small knife secured in a belt loop and sawed at a coconut until it was severed enough to twist off. He looked beneath him to make sure the space below was clear, then dropped the coconut to the ground. Soon he cut off a second coconut in the same manner.

"It makes such a loud thud, doesn't it?" Lois remarked.

"It can kill you," the president explained. "One of my pigs was sleeping under a tree once, and a coconut fell on his head. It fractured its skull just like a small anvil."

"Why did your son get the coconuts for us from that tree instead of the first one he was at before?" Lois asked further.

"To make coconut wine," the president explained, "we must remove the coconut at a proper time, while the milk nectar—I don't know the word in English—while there is a flow. If the coconut is still there, the liquid goes into the shell hollow of the coconut and collects. That's what is happening now. See? The man there opens up the coconut to get to the meat and the milk. It is clear, sweet liquid. Some say coconut water."

The president pointed at a man hacking at the top of the two coconuts with a machete. The president's son then brought us the coconuts.

"As he opens the coconut, fresh, sweet milk, or water, comes out," the president said. "James loves it, but not our tuba."

"Tuba is so sour." I puckered at the thought of it. "If you get it the first day, it's still pretty sweet. But usually they only bring it down from the tree after it's already turning sour."

"That is the best stage of fermentation, after three days," the president said.

"So," Lois mused, "the tuba liquid collected at that first tree your son was ready to get is that coconut water coming from the glands of the tree. Sort of like molasses from a maple tree. This water would collect in the coconut shell, but you siphon it off into a bamboo jar instead. That's what I see up there in the tree top, I think, some kind of bamboo jug or jar."

"Yes," the president said as he smiled at her intelligence. "Would either of you like mango?" the president then asked. "The mango tree is even easier for my son to climb. We have a tree in the back. A very big one. Many mango now."

"That would be lovely," Lois said.

"Sure," I seconded.

The president barked further instructions to his son, who then scampered off.

"You have meat for a change," I said as I took a bite from my plate. "Usually I'm just fed catfish."

"The meat is just for you. We killed it special for you. Also your friend Lois with you."

"Don't do that," I said showing embarrassment. "I'm just here along with everyone else. Don't show me extra favor."

"But we killed our dog for you just like you asked before. He was just a puppy when you said to it, 'You're next.' So now he was fully grown and so we killed him this morning for you like you asked us to do."

Did I miss something in the translation? Filipino to American? Did he somehow misunderstand about "You're next, dog," or did I misunderstand just now about how I ate a dog?

Now I was paralyzed. I had just eaten a dog that was killed because I opened my big mouth when I first got here. This time yesterday that precious dog was alive, but now it was not only dead but being eaten. By me.

And by Lois because of me.

How was I going to finish my meal? But I was going to do it. I was sure dog was not a kosher food. But that dog died for my sins. I was going to do my duty. Somehow. *God,* I gagged inside, *don't ever let me do this again.*

I looked at Lois in desperation. How was I going to get out of this? But the dog was already dead. And dead because of me. Me!

In spite of herself, a laugh at my plight burst out of her.

"You want me to eat it for you?" she whispered. "Since you'll go to hell or whatever happens if you break kosher."

I looked at the dog meat before me, then back at her. I wanted to make a joke to ease the agony, but couldn't. "I'll eat my share. Thank God they gave some to you."

She took her fork and stabbed hunks of meat from

my plate and placed it on hers.

"Just this one time I'll eat dog meat for you," she said, trying to hold back another laugh at my expense. "I'll ease your pain and eat most of it. But let me tell you. I know you don't believe in heaven the way a Christian does, but if I'm going to help you on this, you hear me out. You owe me, so share my analogy. When you get to the pearly gates and face St. Peter, that dog is going to be there waiting for you."

I got the vision of it and laughed at the joke she made for my emotional state.

"He points at me, right?" I said giggling, following her storyline. "That's the guy. That's the one I told you about. And he's a Jew, too."

Chapter 10

I looked at the map. There was no way I was going due east to Digos, then due north to Davao, on up to Butuan City on the national highway, then cut back due west to get to Cagayan de Oro. Even if that route on the national highway allowed me to take a full-sized bus. It was more direct to go due north from Midsayap. On the map it looked straightforward. My one concern was that the map showed few villages, much less towns or cities, anywhere on that highway due north to Cagayan de Oro from Midsayap.

A Peace Corps Volunteer from a rural bank in Cagayan de Oro, assigned there by the Central Bank, had heard me talk about our computerization efforts in Cotabato City at the bimonthly meeting in Manila. He decided his bank could benefit from getting a computer as well. He was willing to learn from manuals, as I had, but asked if I could spend a few days getting some of their personnel started. I could stay with him in his Nipa Hut in a nearby barangay.

I brought three days' change of clothing for the trip and my bank's computer manuals. By the time I got to Midsayap, where I was to transfer to a jeepney in order to head north more directly to Cagayan de Oro, it was lunch time. As I got off the bus at the marketplace, I noticed a white girl. I knew instantly it wasn't Lois—the girl's hair was wrapped in a bun, and she wasn't nearly as pretty. But I wanted to know who she was. I wondered if somehow she was a new Peace Corps Volunteer.

"I'm a missionary," she said after we introduced ourselves. "I work with the university here."

"I didn't know there was a university here," I responded.

"There are two, actually," she explained. "The other one is Catholic. So what are you doing here?"

"I'm a Peace Corps Volunteer."

"Oh, I meet Volunteers every now and then. How do you like it?"

"Challenging," I said with a smile. "But I enjoy it. I'm so busy I don't think about it one way or the other. But since you asked, come to think of it I like it."

"Some Volunteers don't seem all that busy," she mentioned skeptically.

"You get the gamut," I said, feeling embarrassed she had noticed some not so worthy specimens of PCVs. "Most contribute, while some work real hard, and are very devoted. Some, I don't know why they're here. Peace Corps makes it easy to go home, so they could go home if they aren't up to it here."

"I've met some that wonder about that same thing," she said, "why they're here."

"Yeah. So, what do you do here?" I asked to change the subject. I wondered if she needed to feel superior to us.

"Mostly mission work," she replied. "I use the university as a base. I live here on the grounds. I minister to students, proselytize some with families in the area. I teach a Bible class, too, for the university."

"Where are you from?"

"Abilene, Texas."

"Oh, from the South like me. I'm from Mississippi."

"I knew you had to be from somewhere like that," she said with a laugh. "With that accent."

"Your Texas drawl's not strong."

"My parents were missionaries. They're originally from Texas, but we lived a lot of places, and I suppose that accounts for why mine's not as strong."

"Is it okay for you here?" I asked.

"I like it all right. I've been here a year. I've lived like this a lot of my life, growing up. I feel I have a purpose."

"That's good to hear," I said. "I guess you've seen politics like this and poverty like this before then."

"Maybe I did when I was small," she replied indifferently. "I don't remember anything this bad. As a Peace Corps Volunteer, I guess you work with small farmers."

"Yeah. They're my main clientele. If that's the word to use. Where I'm going now is to help a bank computerize, but mostly I work with the poor. Try to find ways to generate income for them on small farms."

"That's good. I just think it's horrible how poor they are. And how much they have to pay for rice. That's their staple food, and they can't afford it."

I thought about what she said. I had to remind myself she was a missionary, but somehow that didn't explain it.

"The price for rice is low," I explained. "Artificially low. Mandated by law to be below market price. That means that producers, these small farmers and such that you're talking about, don't receive what they could because the price is artificially set low. It even gives them a reason to plant something else if they think they can get as much or more for a substitute crop without working as hard."

"Well, the price of rice needs to be even lower. These people are starving."

"They wouldn't be as poor," I explained patiently, "if they received market price for their produce, which is rice. Marcos fears a revolution, and he fears it's going to start in the industrialized big cities. He has seventy percent of the population, which is rural, starving by keeping the price of food artificially low. They're already poor, but this makes it nearly impossible to make a living. And with his cronyism and taxes, meaning his cut of things, industry is struggling too. So these rural poor have nowhere to go. They're stuck on the farm. But as Marcos keeps the price artificially low, it takes away some of the pain in the cities. Or at least he hopes so. I was never more a capitalist than by coming here and seeing how government intervention screws things up."

"Well, I just think it's pathetic how much the poor have to pay for food," she repeated, unfazed by my explanation.

I looked at her, trying to hide my distaste. It was like talking to a liberal. There's something about moralists in general, I decided. One more try.

"It's the rural poor that grow the food. Meaning the rice. They don't buy much, they sell it. If they could get more for their produce, meaning rice, they wouldn't be as poor. They eat from what they grow, they don't buy that much."

"Well, they can't buy much rice because they're so

poor," she said. "If Marcos lowered prices they could buy more. He's just protecting the rich. He doesn't care about anyone but himself."

"I have to go," I said. "My jeepney leaves soon, and I have a long trip. It was nice to meet you. I pass by Midsayap now and then. Maybe we'll meet again."

"Sure, that would be nice." I turned to go and find my jeepney. *And I hope I never see you again.* It was so good to see another conservative, until reminded now how it wasn't.

Perhaps it made me more open-minded, I hoped. To be equally disgusted with moralists of all persuasions. *Moralists drive through the void in their vehicles of clichés*, I thought defiantly.

I went as far as the jeepney took me. To the end of the road. I thought back to the map. I was sure there was a line on that map crossing the interior. But there were no more roads from here. That's why people took the national highway, I supposed. It was the only through road. But for now I was still filled with principle. I was not going to take the national highway and go on a rectangular circumference for anything.

"How do I get to Cagayan de Oro?" I asked the jeepney driver who brought me here to this dead end.

"You must go to Cotabato City and take a boat, then a bus. Or to Midsayap and take the bus on the national highway. It's a full-sized bus. Very nice."

"No, from here, I mean."

"There is no transportation from here," he answered. "Except this same road back to Midsayap. Even if you had a car, there is no road."

"So, I'll walk. Where is the direction? Where do I start?"

He looked at me in disbelief. "Get in the jeepney," he said. "There is a path through the rainforest."

There's a path? I sighed in wonder. *A path? That stupid squiggly line on the map was a path through a rainforest.*

The driver took me until the one-lane dirt road we were on ended. Right at the edge of a rainforest, just like he said. But I loved the idea of walking through a rainforest, as I stared at the trees and vines. I'd never walked through a rainforest before. I had ridden through parts of one in Mexico, but our bus didn't enter it.

"How far does this path go before it reaches a highway?" I asked.

"About ten miles," the driver answered. "No one travels it much. I am not really sure. The rainforest ends, and the path leads to a small dirt road like the one now, and soon there is a village with more transportation. Good luck, my friend."

Tropical rainforests are beautiful. Tall canopy tree rooftops, vines, bushes, flowers, streams. And animals. Birds I couldn't see but could hear in abundance. Monkey screeches like in a Tarzan movie. The only animal I saw up close was a large iguana. It saw me, too, from just off the trail, but was unconcerned.

I was glad when the trail ended, but only because I had so far to go, and it was taking forever. This seemed Biblical to me, in the sense it was a search. Not a safe, structured journey, but a journey with a goal. No set itinerary except a vague, determined destination, and what it took to attain it. On a path through chaotic paradise.

The path out of the rainforest soon led to a dirt road

that led to a village. Just like the man said. A village with a jeepney. I asked where I was, but no one spoke English. People communicated to me that I was now in Lanao del Sur. A Muslim province. I expected to be in this province, the one on the map as predicted, so was encouraged.

The jeepney ride got me to a bigger village on the gravel highway going toward Cagayan de Oro. This village even had a passenger bus, the kind found on the Davao highway, though smaller and older.

"Do you speak English?" I asked a small, bent, wrinkled man smoking a cigarette. He wore a dirty, blue bandana as a head cover.

The man nodded while holding up his thumb and index finger slightly to indicate he understood English a little bit.

"Cagayan de Oro," I said slowly and clearly. "Bus."

He motioned for me to follow, then led me to a bus nearby. "Here," he said.

"Thank you," I replied.

"Where are you going?" a young man on the bus asked from a window of the bus.

"You speak English," I said.

"I went to college," he explained. "I learned there. I worked in Cebu for awhile, too, and picked some up."

"I'm trying to get to Cagayan de Oro," I said.

"You have a long way to go, but this bus will get you on the highway that goes there. But it does not leave until tomorrow morning."

"Aha. So, is there a place I can stay?"

"You better stay on the bus," he said. "If you stay in a lodge, the bus will fill up and you cannot get on it.

It's only half full now. You should find a seat now or it will be gone by dark. Get something to eat and use the restroom. Do not eat much or drink much. You will have to protect your seat and sleep in it. If you leave even to use the restroom you will lose it."

I took his advice and didn't eat or drink anything the rest of the day. While in the village, I found a toilet, then returned to the bus to get myself a seat. I spent the night sleeping upright in it. The bus departed just after sunup the next morning. I slept until we reached a village with a bus that would take me the rest of the way to Cagayan de Oro. On the next bus, I rode on the roof part of the way, since all the seats on it were taken. A lone white American riding exposed on top of the bus going through a Muslim province. A woman asked if I was scared. I said no. It was the only option I had. To not be scared. Soon afterwards, enough passengers got off that I was able to get a seat inside.

I knew the name of the bank in Cagayan de Oro where my friend worked, and that's where I headed as soon as I arrived. I saw one of the clerks looking at me when I walked in the door.

"Are you the Peace Corps Volunteer we've been waiting for?" she asked me.

"Probably," I responded.

"Wait just a moment, please. Everyone is in the back office."

I walked to one side of the entrance and laid down my belongings. Soon, my bank PCV friend and a short, stubby man appeared. My friend's face turned to surprise, then bewilderment when he spotted me.

"I was going to comment, *look what the wind blew in*," he said, smiling as he held out his hand in greeting.

"But you look more like a castaway. What happened to you? We were expecting you yesterday. I've been cooped up here instead of out in the field with our clients. We were afraid you changed your mind. But I guess the worst happened, going by the looks of you."

"Yeah, well." I shrugged apologetically. "I'll tell you the gory details, but first can I shower and take a nap? Maybe shower, a cold beer, and a nap. We'll talk on the way."

"This is my supervisor," my PCV friend said, introducing the bank owner. "The computer is at his house. That's where we'll work. He has that Filipino clone. That's what you said your bank has."

"I brought my manuals just in case you haven't bought yours yet," I explained. "I'll need to take them back with me. And I brought diskette copies of our word processor, spreadsheet package, and database package. I brought some floppies of spreadsheet formulas and macros on spreadsheet, and some programs for the database I've written. That'll get us started. We can talk about it. Mostly, I'll show you what to look for in the manuals, things to make your priorities. They're user-friendly manuals. After I leave, you can start from scratch and do what you need."

"Let's get you cleaned up," my friend suggested. "People will wonder who this vagabond is. There better be some stories behind the mess called 'you' right now."

"You can believe that," I said with a laugh.

"I'm sure I can, Mississippi. You're living up to your reputation. Watch out, Cagayan de Oro, the Marines have landed."

Chapter 11

It seemed as though I hadn't seen Lois in months, when in reality it was a couple of weeks. I couldn't remember the last time we'd spent so long apart. Which was why I didn't want to fall for someone in the first place. The feeling of obligation. And I felt that way because of me, meaning my feelings for her, but I knew she felt the same.

When she came to see me that first weekend after I returned from Cagayan de Oro, it seemed more like seeing my wife again. Seeing her satisfied the longing from missing her. No more empty gap inside. Within five minutes of being together, it seemed like we'd never been apart.

"I want to see more of the world," I explained casually between bites as we sat at our favorite carindaria, "but mostly I'm hoping to get to Hawaii someday. When our time's up, I'm booking my flight for Honolulu and looking for work—if I don't arrange something from here somehow. Trade a third world tropical setting for an American tropical paradise."

"Just stay here the rest of your life, slick," she said. "Hire yourself out to a multinational or to an agency like Save the Children."

"Lois, I've only got so much of this line of work in me. One of the reasons you and I are such good friends is that we want to make a difference here. I feel just as strongly as you about helping people who are down and out. But I couldn't do this forever. We're talking burnout. And I don't mean room temperature beer. I'm talking culture shock. The mindset. I don't blame the International Monetary Fund or the World Bank one iota for their stiff policies. That's what's needed here and in most third world countries. Fiscal responsibility. Doing what it takes to pull yourself out. All this third world stuff just keeps going and going. It feeds on itself."

"People talk about you for saying things like that, Mississippi." She sighed. "You're the only one in the whole Peace Corps who is for the IMF."

"They talk about me anyway, Lois. So much for open-minded liberals. Nice to know the state of Mississippi isn't the only place that stereotypes."

"You back it all up, though, when you talk trash like supporting the IMF. I bet you're a Reagan supporter."

"Glad I don't need a bumper sticker for the car I don't have."

"Aren't Filipinos poor enough for you?" Her frustration showed. "I hate to think what I'd be doing right now if I hadn't gotten the grant that got me into college. Give somebody a break, Mr. Banker."

"Yours wasn't a grant so much as an investment, Lois. There's helping people help themselves, and there's throwing money down a sewer."

"You haven't seen how desperate these people are."

"Yes, I have. I work with them every day. It reminds me of parts of Mississippi, to be honest. Except, somehow, even worse."

"It's worse than that, and they're stuck."

"There's one way out of here, Lois, and I don't mean a ticket to America. I mean learning fiscal responsibility."

"You've been working in a bank too long. In my barangay, people can't get loans. They're lucky to have food."

"We give loans to people in your barangay, Lois. You have a cooperative there, the one where we ate the dog. Don't pretend otherwise. Uncollateralized loans for the riskiest clientele, loans that seldom get paid back. I guess that's a grant, but we didn't intend it that way."

"Maybe it should be a grant," she barked. "The big farmers here own less than twenty acres. Most farmers own less than three. How do we expect these people to survive, much less pay back a loan?"

"Lois, we've been over this," I said, showing my own frustration. "I was there with you last year when that Australian agency talked to the village leaders about the earthen dam. They said the same thing, including the analogy of throwing money down the sewer. Even the grants get corrupted. Even rich countries have limited resources. I know you don't believe that. Things have to work or it's a bad idea no matter how it sounds on paper."

I could tell she wasn't convinced.

"You told me how you babysat to make money growing up, while some of your friends and some of your brother's friends sold drugs," I lectured her. "How you helped support yourself in college as a waitress, or as a student worker. Your brother, you said, had friends who are dead now, and some of your friends are crackheads, while you're accepted into Berkeley Law School. It takes what you did, not what they did."

"You're white, from Mississippi, with a daddy who is a doctor," she said, getting testy. "You don't know what it's like."

"The hell I don't! My grandfather owned a corner grocery, and the only reason my father was a doctor was because of the G.I. Bill after World War II. For services rendered fighting the Japanese. He would have been one anyway—he's a survivor. He makes things work. Plus they had quotas against Jews in those days. He had to get past that, too. And even if my family was rich and had it made, so what? It doesn't change reality. People still have to pull themselves out."

"Don't come at me with your economics," she snapped back. "I took some courses at OSU. I've heard it until I'm going ape. I just know it was President Lyndon Johnson that gave the poor a chance."

"How does having a vibrant economy not give the poor a break? The poor had more chances in a market-oriented economy than anything the Job Corps did for them under LBJ," I snapped. "None of LBJ's programs worked, if you look at the results in context. Higher taxes stolen from the private sector for artificial but visible programs inflicted by government doesn't help industry and the wealth creation process. For all those billions of dollars he totally wasted, he got minimal results. He should have just let the private sector keep it, and real prosperity would have occurred even more so, and the poor would have benefited more from that than from the handouts they barely accessed. With a vibrant economy there is less need of poverty programs and more wealth available to help the helpless."

Lois all but sneered at me. "I hate to throw the race card into all this. But here's this white guy from Mississippi not wanting blacks from Mississippi to get any federal aid. Capitalism didn't help them very much, now, did it?"

"What happened to blacks in Mississippi was not capitalism, it was racism. It wasn't exploiting cheap labor, which I'm for, it was suppressing the market through blind social bigotry. Mississippi hurt its economy, not to mention its society, with unfair laws thwarting drive and talent. Manmade laws sucking the air out of God-given opportunity that provides for a wealth-creating mechanism at the marketplace. Just shows that mixing politics with economics works as well as mixing state and religion. It was Jim Crow laws, let me emphasize the word 'laws,' manmade laws, that hurt blacks where I grew up. Laws that set them back to keep them out of a thriving economy. Laws made to keep them on the plantation and out of the marketplace of opportunity and ideas. And a lot of Mississippi still isn't thriving because of those same laws. They hurt even the people hoping to be kingpins from these stupid laws."

"Say what you want," she countered, "it makes the poor bitter."

"Well, people will stay bitter," I replied, "because they're going to stay poor with that mindset. Our interest rate at my bank is sixty percent. Outrageous, huh? Otherwise, they get money where they always did, if they get it at all, from Chinese traders who charge three hundred percent. And these traders collect their loans, whereas ours are defaulted on by many. So, you tell me. Liberals like you never like the marketplace, but this is the true cost of money, and the marketplace deals with it truthfully. Those that pay back our loans get more below-market-priced loans from us. They get cheaper money and learn responsibility, too. They have a larger success rate than those without loans or those stuck with the traders. Funny how the hell that works, speaking of the IMF. We give loans vastly under market value, and you're still bitching, and we still can't collect from those that choose to lose. They're stuck with the reality they insist on keeping."

"Typical!" She angrily shook her head while refusing to look at me. "Everyone brings poverty on themselves. They're just lazy or stupid. You're so simplistic, Mississippi."

"Give me a break. I've heard this stuff. You're the one that's simplistic. There's poverty until you create wealth. Just like the natural state of the universe is chaos. There's chaos until order is created somehow. Created is the key. Get it? So, you may have bad luck, you may be lazy, you may be stupid, you may not know how. But until you create wealth, there's no wealth. And the best mechanism for wealth creation is the free market. You can't even redistribute wealth if you don't create it. The free market is the golden egg, if there is a golden-egg-laying goose to be had at all. It provides the mechanism. And the losers I brought up to you in this example are the ones who chose to lose, because that's what the bank is going through now. We provided the cheapest credit available, and so many even of the small farmers who cooperatively own the bank have chosen to abuse it. And are stuck without our loans now."

"The Chinese merchants are bad," Lois conceded, as if throwing me a bone.

"Where've you been, Lois? Look at the people you try to help. We feel so proud to give them charity and then don't give the one thing they need, just like with the blacks in Mississippi. Opportunity. Let them work their way out instead of denying them by our protectionist laws. Teach them responsibility. Teach them skills. Give them a break, not a handout. I'm even for a few handouts for those that really, seemingly can't."

"You've made a science out of being a redneck," she said. "Is it a major at Ole Miss? I thought Jews were liberals. You sure you're Jewish?"

"Heard of Milton Friedman?" I returned. "He's as Jewish and as free market as they come, but liberal in the classical sense, meaning looking for answers through an open mind. Not as some political, left-wing dogmatist."

"Yes, I've heard of Friedman. Nobel Prize-winning Economics professor at the University of Chicago. I studied him and Thomas Sowell, also from there. I had to in order to get my Liberal Arts degree. They're just up the road from Ohio, you know. I'm surprised you heard of them down South in hillbilly heaven."

"I thought I'm supposed to be the narrow-minded bigot," I scoffed. "Being from the South. All your harping got this conversation going. Studying them isn't learning from them, and they make sense. They obviously were over your head."

"Listen, Mr. Banker. The high school class where I teach will graduate soon. These kids don't have the slightest idea what they're facing when they leave school. They just think they're going to marry and raise kids like their parents did. I want you to talk to them."

"About what? Banking?"

"That you work for a bank and are interviewing them for a scholarship. But there's a catch. You have one scholarship to offer. Ask them why they are the one worthy. I want to get something through to them. How hard it is in the world. They know poverty, but they don't know about getting out."

"And maybe spend the night at your Nipa Hut?" I hinted. "Like the last time you found an excuse for me to visit your site?"

She laughed and pushed me away while pretending embarrassment. "Yeah, like every excuse I can think of to get you over to my barangay."

"The locals aren't gossiping about these visits from me?" I asked with a chuckle. "*Tsimsis*, as they call it. 'Rumor,' in English. Scandal, by any other explanation. Aren't you scandalized when I show up?"

"The locals are attentive to see if they can detect what we're saying," she said. "Or any other noises that come out of my hut. But they understand we're American. Just like your town does. We're better than a Hollywood movie to them. So scandal's not the word they use. 'Entertainment' works."

"So, kiss me, then," I dared. "Right here in front of God and the ghost of Lapu-lapu, their great chief that killed Magellan."

She stared for a moment, then eased toward me before grabbing my neck and pulling me toward her. Her juiciest kiss yet. I kissed back. Then we embraced tightly and kissed again, not satisfied until sure that what we were doing was scandal to the rest of the carindaria.

****

As much as I thought I was used to poverty, Lois' village never failed to catch me by surprise. Always some new aspect of it appeared with each visit. Sort of like watching a movie again, or rereading a story. On the visit for the bank scholarship interview, I saw a baby with a bloated stomach from malnutrition or worms. There seemed to be more rotting structures not being repaired. Puddles of filthy drinking water used to bathe in or drink from by a family, shared with a carabao. A poverty beyond anything anyone can grasp. Like trying to fathom what a light year is.

But there was always the uplifting joy of seeing Lois' anticipating body leaning out of the window of her Nipa Hut, knowing the jeepney arriving now should be the one with me at this time of day. The look on her face witnessing my arrival and the enthusiastic wave of both her arms directed my way never failed to excite me.

Almost as a ritual we got her water from the hand pump at the edge of her side of the village. In typical fashion, the village stared out their windows to watch us in a procession of two. Their Americans.

"Hey, Filemon," Lois greeted the small friend she tutored as he entered her hut after we returned. The boy smiled. "Supper's almost ready," she said before turning back to her skillet. "Tilapia today," she said describing the menu for supper. She then began talking to the boy in the local dialect.

He smiled at her and sat himself at her dining room table that doubled as a desk.

"Have you done your homework?" Lois asked him, using English again as a courtesy to me.

"I'm having trouble with my math," he replied.

"You brought it with you, right?" she asked.

"Can we do it tomorrow? Or even Sunday? Tomorrow's Saturday, and we only have school in the morning. I don't need it until Monday."

"Since I have a visitor, that's all right," she replied. "The two of us want to chat anyway. After supper, just go back to your parents."

"Hello, Mississippi," Filemon finally greeted.

"Thanks for having me, Filemon," I answered politely.

Filemon was shy, and I almost forgot about him as Lois and I talked. He silently ate from his plate after he sat himself in the windowsill. Quietly he went to the grill for another helping when finished. Putting his empty plate in the sink made more noise than anything else he did. Then he was gone.

"Why don't you get him a chair?" I asked her after he left.

"He has one, but you use it when you're here. I don't bring it up because I like you here. I don't want you worrying about it. You're not here enough to bother with another chair. I had the same problem when the other boy came to be tutored or eat at the same time. I would just stand while I worked or ate with them. Sometimes one would sit in a windowsill instead. They're used to it. Kids here are part of a big family. They have to share a one- or two-room shack, with never enough furniture. So half the kids are sitting on the floor, while some get the luxury of getting to sit on a windowsill. At our school there aren't enough desks in all the classrooms and some of the kids sit in windowsills there, too."

I listened and tried to absorb all she said. I

remembered kids sitting in windowsills as I rode by on a jeepney at times, or as I walked by a structure. I had thought it was just kids being kids.

"Where's your bicycle, by the way?" I asked. "I thought maybe you lent it to Filemon. It's not chained to your post downstairs."

"It got stolen," she said. "When I came back from a weekend with you the last time, it was missing. The neighbors said that very Saturday night I was gone, the NPA came and took it. Hacked through the post to get it. When the neighbors saw the damage the next morning, they got a new bamboo post and fixed the damage for me. They're sure it was an NPA raid, but you never know. It happens now and then. They pass through collecting involuntary taxes."

"Are you safe here?" I asked her, frowning from concern.

"Safer than you," she replied. "You're all over the countryside. Susceptible to ambush. There's never murder here. Just occasional theft. Excuse me, tax collection."

"Whatever happened to the other one?" I asked. "That other boy you were tutoring besides Filemon."

"The older boy?" Lois mused. "I told you how I gave him that money to buy his books and he bought food."

"Yeah."

"That was his attitude about everything. He was smart, maybe smarter than Filemon, but no vision. No sense of sacrifice. I understand hunger. This whole village is hungry. But he knew I would feed him when he came back from town. I think he got excited seeing all the things he couldn't have here. Anyway, I told him not to bother coming anymore."

"Getting to be a hard ass, aren't you?" I smirked. "You sure you're not from Mississippi?"

"Actually, you've scored some points with me," she answered. "I've always been a hard ass, to be honest. It takes some of that. I've seen what it's like to not have a chance, what it does to you, to whole groups. I want to give people a chance, but how? I'm quite stuck with these limited resources you keep harping on. There's an urgency to save the world, but I just don't have enough resources to do it. Not enough of me, or money, or patience, or supplies, or anything. I'm sick of blaming the rest of the world for what's lacking here. More and more it's me, me, me to turn things around here. I have to focus on that."

"When did this transformation take place?" I asked.

"I haven't really transformed," she replied. "But something just happened and I'm still stewing over it. So some of your redneck came to mind lately. I don't necessarily agree, but you did score some points."

"What happened?" I asked.

"Remember that loan the Australian agency gave for that dam project? The one you witnessed and got off to them talking like you about throwing money down a sewer?"

I nodded yes.

"I helped get that loan, as you know. It wasn't much, because the dam they built was a reinforced earthen dam and they used local labor. But it was a lot of money for these people. And their credibility was just about spent, as you recall. They never returned most of the money lent them before on other projects, and the Australians decided they probably couldn't be trusted. And like with your damned IMF, accountability matters to this agency."

"Surprise, surprise," I mocked. "Even with grant money from rich countries, Lois, resources are limited. And poverty and desperation are worldwide. You have to give it not only to those in need but to those who understand about responsibility and doing what it takes. Otherwise aid barely helps out one time, and then it's gone. And helping in desperate times has its place, but in most cases you have to worry about a dependency mindset. There's so much to turn around, and it's not just material needs."

"I went around with the village leaders," she continued, "and the Australian organization. We went to every single villager affected and had them all but sign a blood oath to pay back the money. Every cent."

"Great," I said approvingly. "That's what it takes. And follow-through. Y'all talked about that the night I was with you and the mayor."

"They got the follow-through, too," she said. "We collected every penny. The irrigation it provided created an extra harvest. The villagers were so proud. It was fulfilling. I thought of you."

Her pause let me know there was an epilogue.

"We gave the money to the mayor," she explained further, "who was to give it to the Australians personally. But he pocketed it, I just now found out. He fixed up his house. Even used some for cock fights. I thought he was using money from extra harvests, but it was the loan money we collected."

So many of my own experiences were like this, but my heart sank anyway.

"There was a riot when we found out," Lois continued, "and they almost burnt his house down. But the final result is, he'll probably even be re-elected. He's a Marcos crony."

"You've inspired me for tomorrow, Lois. Not that I needed it. I'm going to be rough on your students tomorrow. I want to get something through. That's what you wanted me here for this time, and I'm ready."

"So, my dear," she said, "you've got carte blanche. We're supposed to share their culture and present ours. I think their little horizons are about to be broadened."

She looked at me meekly. Approving, but resigned.

"Lois," I blurted out to suddenly change the subject. "After the interview with your students tomorrow, I'm going to see Margaret, Rhonda, and Jennifer at their regional capital. I want you to come with me. You have tomorrow afternoon off anyway. And you won't be crashing our party."

She nodded approval and went back to cooking. Her demeanor got more serious by the minute. Suddenly she put down her spatula, turned to me, placed her head on my chest and held onto me for a few seconds. Then just as abruptly she faced me, pulled me down forcefully to her, and kissed me deeply, holding onto the warmth of our tenderness. As if our kiss renewed assurance she needed, she gently laid her head again on my chest, but more as sharing affection rather than demanding it.

The next morning I had added vigor about the task at hand with Lois' students. Before last night, the caring for our Filipino extended family was mixed with a sense of duty. Duty to do what we could, as all but insignificant PCVs, trying to turn around a third world setting. But now duty seemed trite. Now there was urgency.

As I walked with her to the school, I wasn't hardened as much as determined. I knew what to expect from her students, and I intended to be ruthless. I wanted them to remember their meeting with me for the rest of their lives, and if a real opportunity ever approached them like the one Lois and I were simulating, I wanted them to be ready for it. I knew they would not be ready for me. I was so proud to be from Mississippi. It was more the Mississippi in me than the banker that was going to confront these kids.

They were so young. Virtually none of Lois' students would have the opportunity to go to college. It wasn't just a lack of money; they weren't prepared socially or mentally for what would await them at a place of higher learning.

They had a pride about them, though. No matter how poor a family was, they were well kempt. They showered, and their clothes were clean and pressed. Pressed by ironing them with coconut shells and stones. The girls wore cotton dresses, and the boys wore khaki pants and a shirt.

"Good morning, sir," the boy said as he entered the classroom alone to be interviewed by me. He then looked over at Lois, who sat next to me as on a panel, and smiled. "Good morning, Lois," he said shyly. Lois smiled back and nodded, then put on a serious look. The boy immediately looked back at me nervously.

"Good morning," I greeted before looking down at his profile to get his name. "June? Is that your name?" I asked. It stands for Junior, I was told. "How are your grades?" I asked him in a businesslike tone.

"I am passing, sir."

"Do you know why I'm here? Do you understand what this is about?"

"You are going to send me to college," he replied.

"No, that's not it," I answered sternly.

Lois said something crossly to him in dialect. The boy squirmed before looking back at me.

"I represent a bank, and we want to help underprivileged children like you. But we only have one scholarship to offer. Only one. And even then, only if we can find someone qualified."

"I am passing, sir."

"I see you only make Cs," I said in a near monotone. "That's not good enough. It would be hard to find a university that would take you with these grades. Why should I give our one and only scholarship to you?"

"Because I'm poor, sir."

"Everyone in your village is as poor as you. You make only average grades. Is there anything else that might give you an advantage over the others?"

He squirmed more as he thought. "I am poor, sir. If I don't get this scholarship, I cannot go to college."

"I want to help you, but I have only one scholarship. Can't you help me out? What sets you apart from the others to earn this one scholarship?"

"I am poor, sir."

"That's it?" I asked, showing my distaste.

"I have no money, sir."

"Thank you," I said crossly. "I don't believe we're interested in you."

He looked at me in disbelief. *Just like that*, he seemed to think.

The warm smile on the face of the next applicant, a girl, quickly turned uneasy as she saw my serious look and sat down. Lois offered little consolation as the girl glanced at her.

"Do you know why I'm here?" I asked her as I had the boy before.

"You are going to give me money to go to college," she answered predictably.

"What are your grades?" I asked.

"I am passing, sir."

"I see you only make Cs. Is there anything else about you that makes you worthy of the one scholarship I have to offer?"

"I am very poor, sir."

"Your whole village is poor, and I have only one scholarship to offer. Why should I give it to you?"

She looked at Lois for support, but Lois remained grim.

"I am poor, sir. I have no money for college."

"If you stay in this village, you probably will stay poor," I answered her. "I only have one scholarship to offer in your entire class. What have you done to make yourself worthy over the others?"

"I am poor, sir."

I showed some impatience. "Everyone is. I only have one scholarship. Only one for your entire class. Why should it be for you?"

"Because I am poor, sir."

"I don't see anything different about you. It won't be you who gets the scholarship. Can you call in the next student as you leave the classroom, please?"

She looked at me in disbelief but seemed grateful the interview was over.

Of the twenty students I interviewed, only four bothered to show reasons they deserved the scholarship. The girl who was to be Valedictorian not only offered good grades but knew what she intended to study and what she wanted with her life once she graduated from college. The determination in her wanted to leap out of her skin.

"I'm going to talk to one of the universities in my town," I told Lois as we prepared to leave after the last interview. "They must have something for your Valedictorian."

"She has a fire inside of her," Lois affirmed.

"Don't tell her what I'm doing," I pleaded to Lois. "She reminded me of Jacob in the Bible, like I was the angel Jacob wrestled. She fought so hard to get a scholarship that doesn't even exist."

"It's called desire," Lois said as she tiptoed over to give a quick peck of a kiss on my lips. She then hugged me, but in a manner as if to rest from a weary day. "She has so much desire. She's such a fighter. I will remember her for the rest of my life, with every failure or fear I encounter. I taught her how to speak better English, how to write better essays, and understand pieces of literature she never before came across. But she's the one who taught me the most. How to win from nothing. She has so much talent, but what I'll remember is how she's so determined. The Philippines will prosper someday because of her ilk. Once they get rid of dictators like Marcos."

I couldn't let this opening go and grinned at her as I spoke. "And all his corruption, and the overimposing, prosperity-thwarting, manmade laws that come packaged with a superstate."

If looks could kill… But I relished her contempt. She soon eased into a smile, and shook her head before looking away.

"I know a guy from Mississippi at this university in town," I said to change the subject. "I taught a course there once. We'll work something out. I'll need you as a reference for her."

"Of course I'll reference her," Lois said. "But, sweets, we better go. The jeepney to Midsayap leaves soon. The last one until late afternoon. Then we have to catch a bus."

"I'm supposed to meet Margaret this afternoon," I said, "but I couldn't tell them what time. I'm not going all the way up to her site. She'll meet me at the station."

"Are her bees still alive?"

"They're even expanding, hotshot. We haven't had a honey harvest yet, though. I need to give her a new queen and some fumigation papers. It's all in my backpack."

Margaret's provincial town was half the size of mine and on a paved highway. This vastly speeded up getting us there.

Something was happening when we reached the station at Margaret's provisional capital. The market square was abuzz and serious. Had there been another political assassination, I wondered?

I searched the tiny carinderias at the plaza for any Americans. It wasn't long before I heard my name called out.

"Mississippi," a girl's voice boomed. I could barely see her curly brown hair in the crowd, but when she saw me looking, she began waving her arms and jumping up and down. "Mississippi," she called again.

"Rhonda," I yelled excitedly.

"We're over here," she yelled pointing toward the center of the market plaza. "Come with me. Is that Lois with you? I'm so excited to see you again, Lois. Thanks for coming."

Lois and I fought our way through the crowd until we reached Rhonda. We all walked together out of the station area.

"It's horrible, Mississippi," Rhonda explained. "There's an epidemic. Some of the barangays have bad water. I'm not sure how, but kids at the schools drank it, and some are already dying. There's panic. They're flooding the hospital and government agencies. Weren't you a nurse before, Lois?" Rhonda asked, looking at her hopefully.

"Oh, no, Rhonda, not me," Lois answered. "I so wish, but it wasn't me."

"An epidemic," I said shaking my head. "It spoiled your holiday, didn't it, Rhonda." I sympathized even under the circumstances, because PCVs guard their time off jealously.

"No matter," Rhonda said. "That's the last thing on my mind, except I'm glad it allowed me to be here to help out in some way. I was a nurse back in Rhode Island. I'm so glad I came." She grabbed our hands to pull us around a building. "Margaret and Jenny are getting a Coca-Cola at a booth. We took turns waiting for you."

Even the slightest attention from a friend always melted me while I was in the Philippines. At our sites we gave so much, and people expected so much. So when even the slightest kindness was given from someone who didn't need help, it felt special.

Smiles greeted us as we approached the other two.

"Mississippi," Margaret called out. "We were afraid you wouldn't show up. And my goodness, you brought Lois. Fantastic."

"I have your queen bee and fumigation papers, Margaret," I told her. "Can you install her so I don't have to go up?"

"Of course," she said. "What do you think of me?"

"Hello, Mississippi," Jennifer said stoically.

"We're scared to drink the water," Margaret explained as she took a swig from her Coke bottle. "It's supposed to be safe. The contaminated water seems to be in the rural barangays. And only the ones by the rain forest, at that. I guess Rhonda told you about the epidemic."

"I did," Rhonda assured.

"Several have died," Jennifer said as she pulled out a cigarette from her bag and lit it. "All children. It seems to be a problem with school children; I don't know why. That's the only common link we know of right now. It just happened. People are freaking out, as you can see. They don't know what's going on."

"You say it just happened," I asked. "Like this afternoon, this morning, five minutes ago?"

"We arrived at noon," Rhonda said. "The first rumors were already floating."

"The panic has been for the last couple of hours," Jennifer explained further.

I looked around, as if looking for an answer.

"Let's go to the hospital," I finally said. "Let's see what they're up against, what they have."

The hospital was up a small hill just beyond the edge of the marketplace. It gave me time to think as we

134

walked. Doctors and nurses were treating small children on the lawn in front. They were so busy I hated to bother them. I noticed a man and a woman, who I assumed were administrators, judging by their civilian attire, sitting at a table in front of the patients. We approached them, and they looked up from their paperwork.

"Are y'all with the hospital?" I asked.

"We are with the regional health and nutrition office," the woman explained. "Can we help you?"

"We're Peace Corps Volunteers from America," I explained.

"You are what?" the woman asked.

"Peace Corps. We're a volunteer organization from America. We're here to help you in any way we can."

"America sent you here? How did they hear about this so soon?"

"We weren't sent here for this, but we just happened to be here and heard about the epidemic. We want to help."

"I'm a nurse," Rhonda said.

"We have many volunteers," the woman said. "I am sure they can use more."

"Is there anything you need?" I asked. "Supplies?"

"The children are vomiting," the man said. "They are dilapidated. Once their stomachs are settled, they will need food. Most are very poor."

"Is there a place I can call Manila?" I asked.

"Inside the hospital," the man answered. "You can get supplies?"

"Probably," I answered.

My cohorts looked at me incredulously. I had confidence I could deliver, thanks to my experience at the bank.

"Can you ask for powdered milk, then?" the lady asked.

"That would just make them vomit more," Rhonda said.

"They will be able to handle it by morning, and there are severe shortages of food. Powdered milk would be best."

"I thought the water was bad," Jennifer quizzed.

"The water is bad only in two areas. We will supply good water. More reason to have powdered milk."

"I'll get it," I promised.

The lady led me to a phone. I didn't know the Peace Corps phone number, but it was easy to get. The Peace Corps had connections, and by dusk a jeepney full of powdered milk was delivered to the agency staff at the hospital. The man and woman were beside themselves with joy.

"We will separate up the milk," the man explained. "We called for vans and people to deliver. We need to keep half of it here."

"For the patients?" Margaret asked.

The man looked uneasy.

"In case there is a shortage in town."

That left us puzzled, and the man saw it. The woman tried to intervene.

"There are shortages everywhere, not just at the hospital and the barangays."

"Where else is there an epidemic?" Jennifer asked.

"It won't all be used for the epidemic."

As we were talking, those helping them with the milk were furiously carting it off to a van. Lois followed them as if with a radar.

"They think we're stupid," she whispered to me upon her return. "Suckers. They think none of us know their dialect, but I do. They're talking about all the money they're going to make from selling all this powdered milk."

"What will you do with the milk you're filtering off here?" I said as I pushed my way to the van.

"There are other needs," the woman insisted.

"I overheard your cronies over there," I said angrily. "You're selling this on the black market."

The man squirmed. "Only half of it."

Somehow we were supposed to understand this is how life worked here. I did understand that and felt naïve for not considering it.

"I didn't get this to make y'all rich," I yelled, my voice cracking with rage.

"Mississippi," Margaret scolded. "Don't make a scene."

"I'm going to do more than cause a scene," I said angrily. "There are children dying in the barangays. We're trying to save some lives right now. You can cheat stupid American aid workers another day."

"Mississippi," Rhonda said curtly. "Watch your mouth."

I looked at the government workers. "You'd better put that milk back where it belongs. I won't stand for this."

By now everyone within earshot was looking at me. My American friends, except for Lois, tried to pull me away, but I jerked my arm free and kept staring darts at the agency staff.

"We're very sorry for this," Rhonda apologized to

137

the Filipinos around, as all my PCV friends except Lois again pulled at me to leave.

"Put the milk back," I repeated as I jerked free again, glad that I was bigger than everyone around me. I could feel my jugular veins bulging.

Reluctantly the staff gathered the powdered milk onto the tables in front of us.

"The Peace Corps should reconsider accepting Southern rednecks," Margaret lectured me.

I could see the humiliation on their faces.

"And ex-Marines," Jennifer reinforced.

Lois supportively embraced my arm inside of hers and walked with me, stoic.

"They're just going to go around the corner and take off with it to the black market anyway," Jennifer advised. "You know that's how it works here."

"They can't be sure we don't have people to follow through and check on it."

"Yes, they can," Margaret insisted. "They can be sure no follow-through will be made. All you did was cause a scene. The Ugly American. In this part of the world, that type of behavior can get you killed."

"It'll get you killed in Mississippi, too," I countered. "It ain't going to be free for them. At least they got challenged."

"Let's go get something to eat," Jennifer intervened. "It's been a long day."

I suspected the rest of the Peace Corps would hear about this and it would reinforce their perception of me. But I didn't care. Growing up a Jew in Mississippi got me used to being odd man out. Being a Jew of history reinforced it. As far as I was concerned, there were all kinds of cultural exchanges going on.

Chapter 12

"So, this is what you were telling me our first night out in Manila," Lois said to me as we ate at my Lola's. "There at the Hobbit House, while we were waiting to hear Freddie Aguilar sing."

"Then you come with us tomorrow," Lola beckoned to Lois and me. "You pass by the museum all the time, Mississippi. Cotabato City has a cultural museum, and it's on the way to your bank. Just a block behind your jeepney path. Why haven't you been there already, if you are so interested in our history?"

"And they even have some shrunken heads there?" I asked in disbelief.

"Yes, of course," Lola explained. "I rented a jeepney for me and the girls tomorrow after mass. We will come home and eat and then proceed to the museum. When I was a teacher, the museum knew me well. They always made provision for me and my students. I know the history so well, and they let us in free on Sundays, since the museum was closed anyway. I could be the tour guide for my students, and so we did not need any of the staff at the museum. Just someone to let us in and then to lock up again when we finished. That is how it will be tomorrow. I am showing the girls here that board with me. They never heard about the headhunters in Mindanao, and they want to see with their own eyes. I hope the shrunken heads do not give them nightmares. You two can piggyback with us. Is that the word, piggyback? Maybe it's tag along, I think. Anyway, it will be a delight for us to share."

As our rented jeepney turned the corner to the cultural museum the next afternoon, I couldn't believe I hadn't known it existed. A nice single-story, part-stone, part-wooden structure with a big sign to advertise the history that lay inside.

I had always pictured Papua New Guinea when I thought of headhunters. It made sense that other places in the Pacific Islands would have such a past, but I'd never considered the Philippines as being one of them. I began to wonder why. It wasn't so long ago the whole world was the Wild West, so to speak.

"Some say there really were no headhunters in the Philippines," my Lola began her lecture to us. "The only documented shrinking of heads was in the Amazon forests in South America. Since the Amazon was part of the Spanish Empire, as was the Philippines, many think Spain created the demand for heads like you see on display here. I was born in the nineteenth century. I heard my whole life that they existed here in Mindanao. I do not know if it is legend or not. Whether fact or invented, it is a part of our culture. Bahala na. It is of no matter. Who cares? Headhunting parties existed, maybe not because of we savages now called Filipinos but because of our so-called civilized conquerors. The heads became trophies. Headhunting increased under the Spanish, I am told. Maybe it existed only then, and into the early days of the Americans."

Lola and the girls looked at Lois, then me, scoping us out one at a time. I came into the museum thinking they had a savage past, but now it was turned around on me.

"The Americans finally stopped the trade," she continued. "It was for tourists, what I heard about it when I was a little girl. But since I am not always sure what is legend and what is fact, I will tell you both, and you believe or not believe what you want."

Lola led us to another display. She gave us time to study the drawings and read the explanations before continuing.

"While we are on the subject of Filipino savages. The aborigines of many of these islands were the Negritos. A few tribes of them are still around. They are small, pygmy-like people. Many of them were cannibals. Many of them today are still very primitive as hunters and gatherers. But no cannibalism anymore. I think. Ha."

She led us to another display adjacent to where we were and continued further.

"It was the Spanish that named these islands the Philippines, in honor of their King Philip. It was Legazpi that first set up colonies for Spain here in 1565. Spain finally unified all the islands that make our nation today. Before the Spanish, there were many little kingdoms. Muslims were already settling here in Mindanao and the more southern islands. The Spanish introduced our blessed Catholic Church. But even as the Spanish decided we were the savages as they named our country for the first time, they did not even have the courtesy to call us their own name for us. Instead of Filipinos, they called us Indians. We were part of the Inquisition of Mexico administration. Can you believe? So I never knew if we were American Indians or Indians from India, who were known to be not so far away. This was a trading post for the Spanish, and they traded with Goa in India, which was Portuguese. So who am I to my conquerors? I don't know if I am of the people of Geronimo, who was alive when I was a girl, or of the great Raj in India. Ha. Crazy colonialists. Do what you want. You own us, right? Ha. A century after colonization began, there were two hundred fifty-two missions in the Philippines, with two million so-called savages converted to the blessed Catholic faith."

"Can you tell us about these shrunken heads, Lola?" asked one of the girls that boarded. "Even if it is legend. How do you shrink a head?"

"Yes, let's get back to the shrunken heads," Lola said, smiling. "Shrunken heads right here on Mindanao, even when I was a little girl. First the skull is removed from the head. Then the flesh is carefully removed. Red seeds are placed under the eyelids, which are then sewn shut. The mouth is held together by pins from a palm tree. Fat from the head is removed. Then a little ball is placed inside the skin to keep the form appearing like a head. The flesh is boiled in water, and herbs are used, and tannins. The head is then dried with hot rocks and sand and is molded. Then the skin is rubbed with charcoal ash from coconut shells. The ash is not just for taking care of the skin but used to keep the spirit from seeking revenge by keeping it trapped inside the head."

"But Lola," Lois interrupted. "Many of the soldiers around still hunt for heads of the enemy even today. Isn't that true? It is engrained in your traditions."

Lola hesitated as if considering what to say, or perhaps to say nothing at all. After musing for a moment, she explained. "We have headhunters even today, it is true, Lois. It is still with us. It never really ended, if you consider this new trend of it since the early days. What happens now, many times, is not cult practice anymore but retribution, not by the avenging spirit of the head but by rival military clans. Retributions against segments of the population. 'Filipino coconuts' some call this. A rice bag filled with human heads. Sometimes they are even carried on jeepneys. Sometimes it is intimidation, but there are still many superstitious and ritualistic Filipinos that use it as a part of dark magic. I don't know. I'm just an old lady. I don't know what to believe when I hear something. Believe, don't believe. I don't know. Many things happen in the no-man's lands. We are here in the neutral zone. Beyond the neutral zones it is not always pleasant. In the past, some say still with the Muslims even now in the south, there was—and perhaps still is—a slave trade."

She looked at the girls in front of her, who were motionless and expressionless.

"Be careful," she warned. "There are evil people. Pray to the Blessed Virgin to protect you. Know what you are doing. Take no chances. Live long and prosperous."

She then looked at Lois and me.

"The same for you two. But especially you, my dear Lois. White-skinned women are a trophy to some. Don't take risks by going where you don't belong."

Chapter 13

In the Philippines, women are considered the most trustworthy with money. Our marketing cooperative preferred giving the proceeds from produce to the wife. Such was the case with loans from our bank, feeling they would use it more prudently for family needs. Because of this, it was the women I talked to in my Samahang Nayon household bookkeeping courses.

"Every time you go to the store, do not hesitate to write what you spent in your household ledger," I instructed. "To the peso, even to the centavo. Payments out will go here in the right-hand column. When you receive a payment, it goes in the left column. If you keep track of payments and income, it gives you a better idea where you stand in your household budget, whether you don't have money to spend, or whether there's money you may have to buy extra supplies. It helps you keep track of your money situation, what you can afford and what you can't. Hopefully, you will have savings. If enough savings, then maybe you don't have to borrow as much. You can tell if you spend too much or if you have money in the black, money more than expenses. Add the left column and find the total, and also the right column. If the left is greater than the right, you have money remaining; if not, you are in the red. You haven't enough money."

I worried about insulting their intelligence, but the

purpose of the meetings wasn't to teach them simple math and simple bookkeeping as much as to get them to keep track of their money in the first place, and to even think of budgeting. It was simple bookkeeping in every sense of the word. The simpler the better, in order to build their confidence so they could do it easily, and that they should.

"Can you sing for us again before you leave?" a middle-aged woman asked me as the meeting broke up. She, like the other women in attendance, bothered to dress up, wearing simple cotton dresses, pressed, and clean.

I automatically brought my guitar to any meeting I attended anymore, because I felt awkward singing a cappella, and I always got asked to sing. I now looked forward to being asked.

"I learned the words to 'Whispering Hope.' Here I notice you often use it as a Christmas song. Back home, people sing it in church all the year round. Beginning September, Filipinos sing Christmas songs already. It's not September yet, but I'll sing it now."

"Oh, thank you," many said enthusiastically. "It is a favorite."

I loved gospel music, even though I'm Jewish. I even loved that Mississippians were so religious. Though a bit too dogmatic at times, especially about how the Jews were displayed as legalists in the New Testament, and how Jews killed Jesus. But I found Christian services easily moving, and it created a spirit I appreciated, too. There was a lot of crossover in Christianity and Judaism, I determined. I closed my eyes, at times, and forgot there was a difference when I could.

The next day was a Saturday, and I went to Lois' village to work with one of the farmers of the Samahang Nayon on the use of the fertilizer distributer that was made especially for this cooperative by IRRI staff. With the extra irrigation from the earthen dam, and now better use of fertilizer, we were expecting even higher yields in the rice harvest. I wanted to check out the status. Maybe check out Lois' status, too, I had to admit.

I also had tilapia fingerlings for one of the farmers and his small backyard fishpond. The family tended to eat the tilapia at such a young age it was hard to breed them. A tilapia got as big as your hand in four months, and that was the age they began to reproduce. But hardly any were left by then, since this family insisted on constantly raiding the pond. After the first month, these small young fish were scooped up in fishing nets, even though they were only a few inches long at this stage of development. The family would catch them, boil them, and eat them like we would eat ears of corn back in Mississippi.

Lois was preparing supper by the time I arrived at her hut. Filemon studied at her table as he waited for his meal.

"I already brought my water in for the day, Mississippi," Lois said as a greeting while I climbed the bamboo ladder to her living quarters. "Do you mind fetching with the five-gallon jugs before the sun goes down?"

"No 'Hello' or 'Love you, darling'?" I teased her. "You sure are taking our relationship for granted, it seems to me."

"Oh, shush, my darling, love of my life," she

teased back.

She turned toward me, tiptoed, and planted a dramatic kiss for emphasis on my lips, then handed me the containers and shushed me back out the door.

"Hello, Filemon," I said as I went back down the ladder.

"Hello, Mississippi," he returned, smiling.

It was the first time I fetched water for her on my own. But I knew my way by now. The feeling of acceptance, even being taken for granted by Lois, felt good too. I loved being at this stage of our relationship. It felt comfortable.

Filemon was gone by the time I arrived back with her water. Lois had just finished rewarming our food when we heard a noise outside. It sounded like chanting.

Lois shook her head as she walked with our plates to the table.

"Sit down," she said, "I'll explain."

The chanting got louder, and now it was coming from all sides of her Nipa Hut.

"They are lovely people." Lois sighed. "That's how you start a sentence before you say but. But."

As the chanting continued, she grimaced before continuing her explanation.

"I told you," she said, "that for my security, me being alone, white-skinned, and a foreigner, people wander in and out of here all the time. But it's more than that. They are very nosy. I used to leave my hut open even when I left. All the time, in fact, except when I board up to go to sleep. I have things I don't want stolen, but mostly I trust them, especially since I'm their guest. They respect guests. Except for minding their own business. Nobody was stealing anything from me, but it turns out they were going through my things. Just to check me out. Not even for drugs or illegal things. Just to find out things about me. What kind of clothing do I have, what kind of pictures. What kind of books."

She took a bite of her food and purposely chewed in a pronounced way. As if to relieve tension.

"They went into my personal trunk, which is under my hammock," she said, stabbing at her food with her fork and sneering while she spoke. "They found some of my Eckankar books, which I had placed among my clothes. Knowing everyone here was Christian, and with our PCV pledge to keep our own beliefs silent, which I fully agree with, I never left my non-Christian books lying around for anyone to stumble upon. However, they snooped on me, and after finding them, the lady two houses down told me she didn't want non-Christian practices in her village. I agreed to put aside my spirituality while I live here so as not to distress anyone. Which means inwardly putting it aside since I do nothing outwardly anyway. I can handle that because I get to fly out of here someday. Meanwhile, some of the families that you hear below us now, and around us, get together occasionally in the evening and hold a prayer group where they pray out loud that I be released from Satan and his demons, because that was how they interpreted the books. Right now, as we eat, they are trying to exorcise away the evil demon of Eckankar. That's why you hear the chants now."

She put her fork down temporarily and looked at me.

"You're here now too with me," she sighed. "Some

of the prayers are for you. Not for our sinful ways, sleeping together in sin, but because you are Jewish. A non-believer doomed to hell. A Christ-killer."

"Reminds me of parts of Mississippi," I said. "At least Lola doesn't do that."

"Are you sure?" Lois asked. "Have your language skills picked up? Every night she has a Bible reading with the college girls in the living room. At least when I'm there. And then they pray. They always end their prayers with a prayer for your Jewish soul not to go to hell. She is the most loving, kindest person, and she does her prayers for you from love, but she prays for your Christ-killing soul, Mississippi. Hope I didn't pop any bubbles with that revelation."

"I can handle that," I said. "She means well. I've had worse in Mississippi. Not everyone prays for my soul. Some still believe in the Crusades. But I thought you were Quaker, Lois."

"Let me update my spiritual resume with you," she replied. "In Cleveland, I was loosely involved in Eckankar, which is an Americanized system of meditation based on Indian Sikh philosophy and the offshoot system called Sant Mat. What attracted me to it was how it exploded the small box of spiritual consciousness that I learned from Christianity. Although I never really belonged to a Christian church, nor have I been baptized, I began a spiritual search when I was twelve years old, and researched the library through a number of Christian writers, with emphasis upon the mystics. I was an unusual child. My mother was afraid I'd run off and join a cult. Anyway, something always kept me from joining Christianity— something about it just did not sit right with me. The closest I came was Quakerism, and when asked what church I belong to, to avoid complications, I always say Quaker. I realize there are many good, sincere people. I don't have a problem with any of that. I just would like the simple courtesy of being left alone. Like you do for me. I can talk to you. Even non-religious friends think I'm weird for any of this, if they find out. They think it is a cult. Not going to hell for it, just not sane for it."

And on that note from Lois, as if on cue, the chanting stopped. We spent the rest of the night recovering in the silence. I helped her wash dishes, we read, we showered, we went to bed.

Lois and I had our own cultural exchange going on, too. Each night together we would lie snuggled and bring up a topic to discuss: Her more liberal view versus my conservative one. It was akin to negotiations of a contract. If we didn't find a respectable common ground, we might not be in the mood to make love. We had to ply our views gingerly or risk our ultimate reward being denied.

"The counterculture," she explained while we cuddled facing one another in her hammock in the dark, "has to renounce gross materialism and consumption. We need a green balance if we intend to survive. If the human race wants to commit suicide, it doesn't have the right to take down the entire planet with it."

I could feel my blood beginning to boil. *Calm down*, I told myself. I had to find a way to get my side out, but this get-back-to-nature naïveté jerked my strings. I took a breath and thought before I responded.

"Okay, Lois. In Judaism and Christianity, we have these primitive paradise origin stories. A lot of religions do. How there was paradise in the beginning and peace with God. Then sin happened, and now we have exile until we work our way back. But even when mankind was small in number, and material wealth as we know it today was unheard of, both people and animals were dying. Dinosaurs ate other dinosaurs, mammals had a food chain, man came along and raped and pillaged other tribes. In our genetic makeup we have instruction to survive. Survive for the sake of life. The species must continue. It's up to the individual to survive for the sake of reproduction, and for the group to survive, too. So we have to find ways to protect ourselves, even to thrive. In our genetically influenced psychological makeup we are given a huge leash in managing our affairs. If we feel threatened, genetic instruction—or at least genetic persuasion—comes out in us. But we have our social cues, too, influenced directly or indirectly by our DNA."

"There you go again, Mississippi. Get to the point. I don't wander all over the place on you. Are we going to make love or not?"

"Am I just supposed to give in to you and make you happy and get serviced?" I asked, showing frustration. "Don't you want our reward enough for us to earn it? Our little talks aren't going to accomplish much if I just give in to you, you know."

"Get to the point for my sanity, then," she whined. "I'm not trying to cut you off. I want to make love too. But you're turning me off with all this philosophical meandering. Is it the Jew in you?"

"Okay, okay. I'll cut to the chase, Lois. The whole universe is a mixture of survival of the fittest. Not by one element killing off another, but strength overcoming weakness. Including by inclusiveness and cooperation. But dog eat dog gets in there, too, if cooperation fails. There are more people on earth now. We seem to have more security and physical betterment, as in more goods, but we'll always have infinite wants. More joy from more food and more entertainment. These people we're with right now in the barangay slash and burn and pollute the air."

"They're trying to just survive," she explained.

"Yeah, survive as an individual, as a family, and as a society. And polluting the earth as they do so. And eroding it. That isn't very green, you know. You act like the industrial world is just this great unjust, blind, rape-the-earth machine. That happens. And other species do it, too. Then on top of that, there are tornadoes and volcanoes, and tsunamis from the volcanoes."

"Corporations on Lake Erie just dumped their chemicals into the lake," she countered. "It got so bad Lake Erie caught fire right there near where I grew up. Corporations are out for themselves. They are greedy and malicious, and the rest of us be damned. They want everyone to work for nothing, and they fire and outsource. My daddy lost his job so they could hire cheaper people in Mexico."

"He was part of a union, and it collectively bargained for wages higher than market value," I countered.

"Don't come at me with this tripe, Mississippi. I want to forget this side of you."

"Don't forget it. Listen to it."

She jerked away. "Aaaaahh."

"Your daddy is equal in the sight of God and the constitution, but not equal as an economic element," I continued. "The marketplace is indifferent, my sweet, naïve darling. That's why idealists hate it. But put your idealism to better use. Work with what produces in this material plane we live in. Because this is how we physically survive. As economic elements. You just look at a corporation as some fat, greedy, selfish cat. As indifferent. It's struggling in the same world you are."

"That's what they are," she sneered. "Fat, greedy, and selfish."

"They ain't rich when they fail. They have to compete."

"They need to have a heart. They need cooperation for the species to survive, you said so yourself."

"They have to survive, and it takes cooperation as well as competition. If they don't make the best product for the lowest price, someone else will, and the consumer, who also wants to survive and prosper, won't buy his piece of junk for that price. No wonder you live in the rust belt, Lois. Nobody gets it up there. The automakers in Detroit used to have planned obsolescence with their cars, purposely making them to wear out quickly, so we'd have to buy another one."

"That's exactly what I'm talking about," she snapped back. "Corporate greed. And they didn't pay their workers diddly-squat while they did all that."

"Because of collective bargaining, they paid their laborers more than their economic value."

"You are a barbarian. And boring."

"No, I'm not. I'm not the one who started buying German and Japanese cars. The American consumer did. Or Japanese steel instead of steel from Pittsburgh. The American consumer did. Once competition entered the formula, our automakers, and our steel mills, and our broom factories, started losing out. They were paying their laborers too much to make an inferior product. Managers and investors had to give up cheating us with planned obsolescence and make a good, if not cheap enough, product. Our consumers chose something else until satisfied. I didn't, the rest of America did. You probably did. When we go to the market and shop I don't see you taking the flimsiest and most expensive barrio buster. You shop to kill."

"These corporate executives sure make enough money," she said. "They make millions, while the little guy barely gets by. And you're taking up for all that."

"Well, the small guy doesn't make the company run. The small guy shows up and puts lugs on a wheel, or does the accounting or engineering, and has job security while doing his small share. The engineers make more than the welders by the way. I wonder why. Welders are important but they wouldn't have much to weld if the engineer wasn't smarter and doing a more important job. So there. This fat cat CEO you hate makes sure the company doesn't go bankrupt. This job security thing you take for damn granted. The fans in the stands don't come to see me quarterback the San Francisco 49ers, they come to see Joe Montana take the 49ers to the Super Bowl and win the championship. He's worth his money. If not, they fire him. Same with chief executives. They've got a company to run, a product that better get built and sold, and a nice hefty profit made for all the workers, the investors, and the governments that tax them into oblivion."

She just lay there. I could tell she wasn't listening. She was hating my guts.

"With competition," I continued, "the corporations

had to make a better product, and they had to make it for less, or the consumer, you, wouldn't buy it. If they don't hire Joe Montana, who charges a high price, they don't win the Super Bowl. And there is a huge difference in Lake Erie now. Competition and technology cleaned it up."

"Yeah," she came back, "after a law was passed to make them."

"If you share a resource, you don't treat it the same way as if you owned it."

"You're suggesting corporations should buy Lake Erie. They'd take good care of it then? Yeah, right. Ha."

"They'd take better care of it than just dumping chemicals in it and letting it die and not have water to drink or fish in. They'd be more responsible about it."

"Tell it to the Marines," she bit out.

I squirmed. "I admit that if their major concern was a cheap dumping ground and they had access to other sources of fresh water, Lake Erie might seem expendable to them. To the detriment of both us and Mother Nature. You got me on that one. Half got. My principal has some merit. It doesn't always work out, though. I am generalizing a bit, I admit. I know there have to be some laws, but speaking of greed—give a politician a cause, and the next thing you know you're so lawed up the fish can't use Lake Erie, either. Anyway, I'm just saying people take care of what is theirs better than they take care of what is collectively shared. In general. So if we have to share a resource, we have to pass a law to protect it equally. And empower our governments while we do it. And those governments are no paragon of virtue, like I just mentioned. With technology, though, we were able to reduce pollution in the air. We'll find more solutions as time goes on, unless we resort to living in caves. Going back to the slash and burn they use here isn't the answer. Because people are going to instinctively survive, as genetically induced, no matter how many laws you throw at them. With a better economy, we voluntarily reduce our family size, increase our education opportunities, and find other things to do than just plant and hunt and fish. You act like only the rich are greedy. Everyone wants betterment."

"Tell it to these people here. You're calling them greedy?"

"They are human. They care for others, but they also are greedy. Just like humans everywhere. We give these poor people loans at below-market interest rates, but they don't pay us back. Instead, they go out and buy a radio. That's greed. I'm not condemning, just saying."

This was the most heated talk we'd ever had. I wondered if I was going home tomorrow biologically unfulfilled.

I turned onto my back and stared upward into the darkness. Waiting. Hoping. I reached over to hold her hand, and she pulled it away. But not angrily. More like "give me time." I waited some more.

"You really believe all that tripe," she said, just above a whisper.

That was another good sign. As if she was thinking and cooling off.

"I'm looking for answers too, Lois. I want answers. Not moralisms."

"Is that what I'm doing?" she asked. "I'm just this airhead moralist? I hear you talk that way about others.

Is that what I am to you?"

"You haven't heard of Maslow's hierarchy?" I countered. "You know, the psychologist? He was basically saying, just like the mission at Mt. Carmel, you can't get to the soul until you get past the body. We're here on a material plane and have to satisfy material needs before the soul pays you much heed. The more basic the condition of depravity the entity faces, the more basic is the DNA response. It takes over instinctively. Even then there is a long leash for that individual entity in what to do. The entity doesn't get a pass on anything that goes to save itself. It still has laws to abide by and ethics to follow, upward seeking to encompass. But it does get more to the chase of survival when it's pushed hard."

"You're getting close to Jewing this up, Mississippi. I liked what you were saying up to now, but you sure do want to overkill your elaboration."

I thought for a moment. I didn't want to lose her.

"In other words, Lois, there's a type of division of labor involved here. There's the material and physical needs and wants, which are infinite in a finite resourced world, and the spiritual, this infinite God-needing thing. Somewhere beyond our most basic physical demands, we start opening up to the spiritual, unless, in ignorance, we stay bogged down in materialism. You've had experiences, Lois. It's formed ideas in you. I see how much you care. Watching you with Filemon tonight melted me. You have a degree in English. I love literature too. It's a teacher. But I have an economics degree. It's not a degree in master race. That was Hitler. Economics teaches us the ins and outs of how to get material things done. Things we need and things that make us more fulfilled in a material way. Literature helps with our souls. These aren't two different entities as much as they are parts of the whole. They need each other. And I need you."

She rolled half way toward me and took my hand.

"And I need you, Mississippi. It looks like we make love again tonight. I was worried for a moment we wouldn't make it."

She rubbed my hand softly and affectionately as we lay in the dark quietly.

"We're genetically geared to compete, but also to cooperate," she said as if in a review session. "For survival of the species. Remember that time we rode the jeepney together going to Midsayap? Where I tried to ride the bumper with you?"

"They wouldn't let you," I reminisced with her. "You're a woman. Women tire more easily, but also, women fall off more easily. Or if there's an accident or ambush, no one wants to see a woman suffer."

"Exactly," Lois said. "Survival of the fittest includes gallantry of the strong to protect the weak. Remember what that man said to me to get me to go inside? He tapped me on the shoulder. That's what they do. They tap on the shoulder and say, *I will be the one*. I will be the one to take the hardship and danger. That is so beautiful, so touching."

She turned fully on her side as if to look at me, even though we were in total darkness.

"When we get married someday, Mississippi, that's going to be our wedding vow. Before you kiss the bride to seal our marriage, we're going to face each other, look each other in the eyes, hold both of our hands, and say to each other—"

She placed her hand on my cheek for emphasis. "Let's say it now. I want to vow it right now. Let's do it."

"I will be the one," we said to one another.

"Whenever one of us is weak," she continued, "the other will be there. We will always be there for each other. We will always survive."

We sealed our vow with a kiss.

Somewhere during the night we heard gunfire. I heard it in my sleep but didn't understand it at first. Then I jerked and sat up. Lois gently pulled at me to lie back down. Was this why they called this region the Wild West?

"It happens," she said. "Is this the first time it has while you've been here?"

"This happens?" I asked, aghast.

"I told you that," she said. "I told you about the gunfire at night sometimes."

"No, you didn't. You never told me you hear gunfire."

"When it happens, it's at night," she explained. "Somewhere after midnight."

"You've got to be kidding."

"Maybe I was afraid you'd act like this," she said. "It's nothing to get excited about. They're in another village. Nothing we can do about it. They're hamletting."

"What are you talking about?" I asked, showing my frustration and anger. I was scared to death for her, just hearing the gunfire. Then I heard there was a creepy story about the gunfire. A common story somehow.

"The elite military forces sometimes conduct

searches in a wide circle. Like documentaries I've seen about Polynesia or somewhere, where the village forms a wide circle and beats on the water to scare the fish in. Then when the fish are close together and convenient for the villagers, they close in on them with their nets. Some of the farmers here do that in the rice paddies to kill the rats. But here, the elites close in on a village, then a hamlet. They go under and around a Nipa Hut so no one can escape. Then everyone is killed. Everyone. Old and young alike, male and female. Since I've been here, it's never happened to this village. I suppose it's used on suspected NPA, but I don't know all who it happens to. Perhaps even political opponents, for all I know. And the NPA does it to a village or family that cooperates with authorities. I try to center myself and hold myself open for those tragic, lost people. In some way I want to be a channel to heaven for them. Maybe, while their soul escapes from this horror, somehow I can help ease them into a channel to heaven. That's all I know to do. The last thing they know in their lives is the horror of a late-night execution and death on all sides."

I was so moved by her thoughts and feelings. This was the purest woman I'd ever met. All she seemed to know in her life was to be there for people. Even for people miles away in the middle of the night, people she couldn't help in any other way except to exude her essence for them. I wanted to believe it helped.

"I timed it last time, and it went on for twenty-five minutes," she explained.

I was horrified for her now. I could see why she hadn't told me about this. I didn't know if I could sleep anymore in my safe little room at my Lola's in

Cotabato City. She had been protecting me this whole time by not telling me. Letting me have peace for her being. I wasn't allowed until now to share this about her, to add it to my fears while I was at my safe abode.

"No one will say a word about this in the morning," she continued. "I don't know if it's superstition or fear. But no one will mention anything. I call these coffin mornings. Before long, we'll see many jeepneys passing along the roads and highways. Either coming for all the coffins or taking them away. It depends on the circumstances. I see more jeepneys and coffins than I actually hear gunfire. I don't really know how many massacres there have been out here. This is the third I've heard at night while I've been here."

"Marry me, Lois," I pleaded. "You already brought it up. Marry me and come live with me in Cotabato City. Away from this."

"Someday," she whispered. "Someday we'll get married, because that's what we want. But for now, my place is here."

Chapter 14

It was harvest season, and the schools were out so the children could help their parents in the fields. What this meant for me was that I saw more of Lois. She had more free time now. It also meant I spent more time in Cotabato City, since she moved in with me during this break. So there was no need to see her at her place on weekends, few as I did anyway. Now she regularly helped me with my projects. And in spite of the inappropriateness of our living arrangement, Lola seemed fond of having her also.

"Why is the dog barking at me, Lola?" Lois asked while we sat in the living room. She was familiar enough with Lola now to allow frustration to show.

"You are a stranger," my Lola replied. "He is protecting me."

"He barks every time I come. I just want to visit with you awhile, Lola. Not just have to immediately go up to Mississippi's room or to a carindaria. He barks at me constantly. If I sit here for an hour, he barks for an hour."

"He still barks at me, too," I said. "I've lived here more than a year, and for more than a year now he barks at me. If I cook and he's around, he barks at me. While I'm eating or sitting in the living room like now. Lola, why am I such a stranger to him?"

"I don't know if it's your white skin," she said, "or

if you have a different smell. But it is good he barks. That way I know he will guard us against robbers."

That didn't cut it. "He'll still guard you if you teach him not to bark at us."

"I'm afraid if I get after him he will relax against thieves too," she explained.

I had been over this with her before, but Lois' complaints brought it back to me.

"It's that way everywhere," I said to Lois, but glad Lola heard. "We have a watch dog at the bank. He barks at me the whole time he sees me. Once I went out to the sidewalk where he was. I sat next to him for half an hour. I wanted him to smell me, or get a better look at me, whatever it took, just so he'd stop barking after a whole year of me working there. He bit me, instead. Then kept barking. I still sat. And he still barked. When I go anywhere else, if there is a dog around, it barks. The one exception was the little puppy dog at that Samahang Nayon that grew up and I ate it. Some kind of karma, I guess, for it being nice to a white guy."

Lois started to say something but decided against it.

"Let's go to Mr. Rancon's," I suggested. "Some of the farmers are there, and they're making soap from coconut oil. They make coconut shell charcoal, too, but it's a by-product from the soap process. I wanted to show you, anyway."

As we rode along in the jeepney, Lois began to relate recent events in her village. She began casually, but the more she released, the more she needed to say.

"It was after the last time I visited you before school was out," she said in a near monotone. She looked straight ahead, out the side of the jeepney away from us, past the passengers, but not directly at any particular thing. The more she tried to be indifferent, the more it portrayed her concern. "I stayed with you later than normal that Sunday, if you recall, because we went to the museum with Lola and the college girls. It got me to Alamada late, and I had to wait at the market for what was the last jeepney ride home. I thought I'd need a tricycle."

She spoke so solemnly I could barely hear her for all the traffic noise. I leaned toward her slightly to hear better.

"There was this American there," she continued. "You and I are the first white Americans these people have seen in decades, and suddenly there's this American from out of nowhere. Doing what? Visiting? Who? A tourist? For what? No transportation or highway that's easily accessible. A bad bridge he had to get around. Was he USAID for your bridge project? Was he lost? What was he doing here? Maybe a missionary, I'm thinking, because that made the most sense. I understood better why all the locals think we're CIA, because here I was wondering what the fuck this guy's doing here."

Her language caught me by surprise. I'd never heard her use harsh words before. Not even after the ambush or the military confrontation in Davao. I listened intently.

She glanced at me sheepishly, as if human again. She then shook her head, blushed, and nibbled on her lower lip nervously.

"Maybe I've been here too long," she said. "I'm paranoid, or at least overly suspicious. Exactly things we think about the locals when they behave like this.

But there was something about that guy."

She smiled shyly toward me yet again, looked down at her lap for a second, then raised her head to stare back out toward the street, past the passengers, as we rode.

"He claimed he was just out of the navy. I guess Subic Bay, but he didn't say. He could speak Tagalog better than me, even knew slang words I didn't, and left me a sheet of verb conjugations. He said he was just winging it through the neutral zone. So that leaves out missionary, I concluded. I had wanted him to be a missionary. I could live with him being here for that. But I'm sure he was some kind of operative. Maybe I'm being paranoid, but I don't think so. He was dressed down, in worn jeans and faded shirt. He was so buddy-buddy with people. But so are you, Mississippi, so I'm still working on that. I've just been here so long and must be turning native in the mind. Anyway, I was having a coffee at a carindaria while waiting on my jeepney, and I watched him get off a jeepney coming from Midsayap. From the national highway, you know. He sees me, this white girl at the Alamada marketplace, and it's natural for him to come over for a visit. I'm curious about him, but in my mind he's still a tourist or something."

The jeepney we rode stopped now, just short of Mr. Rancon's house, to let off a passenger. I was so engrossed with Lois' story, however, I almost missed that we had arrived. I wasn't in the mood to go to the soap factory now. Lois needed me. Was something up, as she feared? And what all exactly did she fear, or was she going native in paranoia, to her detriment, as she feared?

165

"Let's go to a park bench," I suggested. "There's one nearby. Would you like a Coke or something to take there?"

"I'm okay," she replied. "Let's just talk. Find a bench out of the way. People will be eavesdropping if for no other reason than we're *Canas*."

We walked along silently until we got to the park. As we turned toward one of the benches, Lois took my hand to hold affectionately, as she often did. But this time she smiled at me shyly, as if apologizing for doing so.

"He began talking casually," she continued her story as we sat near a flower garden at the edge of the park. She was more relaxed now. "He told me his name, but I'm sure it's a fake name. His casual questions became bit by bit more pointed as to what was actually going on in the region. My curiosity about him turned into suspicion. Or maybe paranoia. So I changed what I was saying from giving any information about where the no-man's land was around Alamada, and who were the targets of the military elites, as well as the NPA's targets. I began telling him the opposite of what I knew or thought, as well as saying things had quieted down, which wasn't true. I decided to Mata Hari him in this damaging game he was playing with me."

"Don't use the word paranoia anymore," I said reassuringly to her. "Native mindset might have seeped into your psyche, but only by making you unsure of yourself. We don't really know who this guy is, but what you're telling me sounds more than suspicious. You're trying too hard. That's good. We don't want to be trigger happy in our assumptions. But this really does sound suspicious, and I'm just listening to you."

"There's more," she said. "It gets bigger."

I leaned back into the park bench backrest. I was ready for the long haul. That's where we seemed to be heading. She leaned back with me.

"My jeepney for my village was boarding then, so I apologized to him and got up to leave. He followed me. I looked at him cynically, but he continued on with me."

"'I enjoyed our talk,' he told me. 'I'd like to see your village and find out more about what a Peace Corps Volunteer does,' he said. He didn't ask me, you know—he *told* me he was following me. I thought about demanding he not do that, but I didn't want to let on how suspicious of him I was by now. I could make a scene, but I couldn't really stop him. So I just warned him that there was no place for him to stay there, that it was a small, impoverished village. Plus, I didn't want my neighbors thinking I was cheating on you. Just his presence with me would do that. I was really bugged with him by now."

She leaned forward, deep in thought. There was tension left, but fight prevailed.

"One of my neighbors indeed saw us together when we arrived. One of them, in fact, who had tried to exorcise the devil out of me that night you were there. You know, when my neighbors did all that chanting outside my Nipa Hut. Anyway, I didn't want this guy following me to my hut, so I went straight for a small carindaria near where the jeepney stops. It's near a church near the square, and this woman was there in the church lighting a candle. When she saw me, she came over, and I introduced them, telling him she was like my village mother, and explained to her that he was traveling through. He asked her about lodging there, which made me squirm even more, because I really was suspecting him by then, especially since I had already informed him there wasn't anything. Now, in my mind, I'm calling him an SOB, because he would compromise me at my site. And here he was, willing indeed to compromise me for information. Well, this lady invited him to stay for dinner and overnight at her house as a guest, which he immediately accepted. I know she saw I was on a spot because here I am socially attached to you. But I was inwardly fuming from all this. CIA is supposed to strictly stay clear of us. If he was not CIA, then being ex-military he still should know better."

"That doesn't matter to a stranded sailor, though," I explained. "I think he was some kind of operative, too, but just saying. A sailor or soldier or whoever, hey, they're going to make a move of some sort. Even if it's to get to you as a social outlet."

"I suppose," she conceded. "Anyway. Meanwhile, he's acting like he's this tipsy buddy-buddy, *barcada* guy who just wants to hang around with San Miguels and shoot the breeze. After dinner he went to one of our few open carindarias. It's after dark now, and only men go out at night to drink. He came back around ten p.m. I was still with this neighbor woman at her place, and she let him in. Then she retired for the evening. I hung around because he acted not just drunk but a step beyond tipsy. He told me about talking with men there and getting a sense of things going on here. Then all of a sudden he was silent, and stared at me like assessing me. Then his voice and demeanor changed completely. Suddenly there's no display of tipsiness, but in a very abrupt, calculated manner he briefly told me I was okay. Like I passed some muster, I presumed. That he'd obtained what he was looking for. He said it in a way like he was committing this recital to memory, as if it was impossible for him to literally write down notes, so they wouldn't be confiscated, or dropped and lost somewhere, thus revealing something. Actually, I don't know that. I just pretty much made up my mind he was doing that."

"Don't you ever use the word paranoid on me again," I repeated to her firmly. "We really don't know, and you can misjudge, but this is no paranoia. This sounds like you were targeted by whoever. Yeah, CIA or military Intel comes to mind. It's beyond an educated guess. Maybe we're wrong, but—naw. This is so in your face."

"He was gone early the next morning," she continued. "Since he came by way of Cotabato City, we talked about the museum Lola took you and me to. It was fresh on my mind, since I just came from there. I asked him if he stopped in the museum there. He said yes. When I arrived today, before coming to Lola's house, I went by that museum to check his story out. I remembered we had signed in when we entered. His name, the one he gave me, wasn't there. So either he lied to sound like a tourist, or he wrote a different name. That same morning before he left to get to Midsayap to go to Davao, he met one of the more influential ladies of our village on the street. She runs a little store here, you know these little roofed stands that sell canned goods and things. The *sari-sari* stores. She told me later that all the locals who came across him were suspicious of him. I know to take that with a grain of salt, but it sure didn't reassure me about him being just a guy seeking American companionship. She looked me straight in the eye, which is unusual for a Filipina, and asked me bluntly what I thought of him. Did I think *my friend*—those words, *my friend,* she called him—this guy I brought to the village the night before, might he be a spy, or not? I had about thirty seconds to make a choice. Should I tell her I didn't think he was a spy, when I did, or should I lie and look like I'm covering up? This so compromised me. She kept staring into my eyes, and I knew I couldn't deceive her, so I told her, yes, I thought he was a spy. And I told her that when he asked me for information I didn't tell him the truth. She seemed satisfied with that answer, and I saw how she also thought he was a spy. I hoped I was going to survive this."

The way Lois said she hoped she would survive this made me think there was an epilogue to this story. A bad one. The way she stared at the ground at her feet intensely as she said it made me all the more sure she had something bad to say.

"A couple of days later, after this SOB came to my village," she said coldly, "our village was attacked by some gunmen, and our small marketplace was burned down. That's never happened before, that I'm aware of. I was relieved I wasn't hamleted. More relieved my neighbors weren't. Was this because of me bringing this man into the village? I can't get it out of my head how it must be that. I don't know what to think. Coincidence, maybe? I'm still trying to remind myself of that possibility, but I have to force that concept down my throat."

"You've got to get out of there, Lois," I said firmly. "Get the hell out of there."

"They're my people." She looked up at me in appeal. Her eyes turned red, her lips trembled. We were in public, but I held her to me while she cried on my shoulder. The summer harvests had come just in time, I decided. Like a manifestation from God. She was here and safe for the next few weeks. But how was I going to get her out of that death trap permanently?

Chapter 15

As I worked with our bookkeeper on a spreadsheet, I felt a tap on my shoulder. I turned—and stared. What was Lois doing here on Monday afternoon? After spending time with me, she had gone back to begin the new school session. She had returned to her village on Sunday, the day before, to get reoriented with her life there and prepare for a new school year. Which is where she should be right now. In school teaching, instead of here.

"The good part is," she explained as we walked together outside the bank, "I spent these past few weeks with you and had most of my belongings with me, including my passport. The bad news is, I don't have a village anymore. Nowhere to go. Someone blew up my house with a hand grenade."

Lois was impressively calm, considering the news she'd just laid on me. The night in her village to contemplate her fate, and the long ride to Cotabato City, had given her time to adjust. As much as one can.

"Where are your things?" I asked her.

"At our Lola's house. In our room. Everything I own is in my backpack. The same possessions I packed yesterday morning when I headed home."

I stared off into the distance, then turned back to look at her as I stuck out my elbow for her to embrace as we walked home. Our home now; we were together somehow.

"My neighbors explained to me that my Nipa Hut was blown up the very day I left to come spend the school break with you," she said. "Did whoever did it know I was gone and this was a warning, or am I supposed to be dead? People in the village did not report the incident to anyone because they didn't want to cause a problem. They are sure it was NPA retaliation for me being a spy. Meaning that SOB guy, even if he wasn't an operative himself, was so blatantly perceived as one, including by me and you, that it convinced others that I was too. I am so furious I'm beside myself. I want to go to the U.S. Embassy right this minute and give them a piece of my mind. But the reality—the official legality—of it all is that he didn't exist. That's what you hear in the movies and on the news, anyway. So, thus, nothing happened. There was no American at my village, or if so, just a tourist. Or that I'm out of my mind. Whatever. You know that's what we're going to hear from them. Probably only a few of his cohorts even know about him to begin with. But whatever. I have no place to live anymore. They're probably going to send me home now. For getting involved. Or for having the audacity to have my place get blown up. And if they find out, and they will, that I spent the last few weeks with you—well, there you go. I should have stayed and planted a garden or something, but I'm sure I accomplished more here with you, including learning the computer you have, and working with the girls doing their ledgers."

"You don't have to convince me," I said sympathetically. "But you ain't going home. Or to a new site. And you can't go back to your old site even if

173

they let you and even if you wanted to. You're marked there. You'd be hamleted. And perhaps your friends there, too, for being involved with you. They survived your hand grenade by not getting one of their own. We don't want to push our luck at their expense."

She nodded her head as if in agreement with what I'd just said.

"You're right. At least I'm the only one they're after. Whoever 'they' happen to be. They've had plenty of time to hamlet others by now. My God, can you imagine if the NPA had hamleted my neighbors because of this piece of crap?"

"Let's get married," I said. "You've lived with me for weeks now anyway, working with me on my projects. You know everybody here. Everyone loves you."

"You'd marry me?" she asked.

I glared my look of anguish at her to portray what I thought was the most ridiculous question I ever heard.

"I'm so sorry this happened to you, Lois, but the crying part's over now, and the future makes me happy. We've already proposed to each other and vowed to vow. So if you need reassurance about my attitude, then, well, my God, here it is. I love you, Lois. I want to spend the rest of my life with the deepest, gutsiest, most caring person I ever met. Marry me. Don't even take anything that happened as some sign from God. Just marry me because I don't want to live anymore of my life without you in it. Get it?"

I turned and walked back toward the bank, opened the door, and stuck my head into the entranceway.

"Lois and I are getting married," I shouted.

There was loud applause and cheering throughout.

"I want to marry you, Mississippi," Lois whispered after the celebration died down and we left again to walk home, "but let me get my bearings on this. Now that it's really upon us."

I rolled my eyes. I knew she was right, and I'd wait. But I knew full well we were going to get married, and soon.

I called Peace Corps Manila that afternoon and told them about Lois and what had happened. Before they had a chance to decide the next step concerning her duties, I informed them that we were getting married. Then I gave the phone to Lois for the details to be ironed out. In an emergency situation like this one, the Peace Corps would pay for a PCVs flight to Manila. Because we were getting married, the Peace Corps agreed to reimburse me for my flight, as well, once—and if—our marriage and site plans were approved.

"It would even save the Peace Corps money," our administration director told us in our meeting after we arrived in Manila, "if you two do get married and Lois is reassigned to work with you at your bank in Cotabato City. I understand your situation, Lois, and I appreciate your attachment to Mindanao. But please don't get married over this. Take time to realize what you're doing. You both have the better part of a year left on your assignment in the Philippines. Don't rush things."

"You can ask anyone who knows us," I said, "how we've been emotionally attached since San Diego. We spend all our weekends together, and our R&R trips, too. We have deep feelings for one another. The only reason we aren't married already is because she loves her village. But y'all won't let her go back, and the next best thing is to be with me. We want to get married.

The sooner the better."

"I believe you, Mississippi," the director said, "but I need to hear Lois verify it."

"Yes, it's true," she said. "That's what we want. That's what I want. I am very attached to Cotabato City already, and his environment. And we do love one another very deeply in every sense of the word."

He picked up his cup of coffee to take a sip, then stared off into the distance.

"I've helped PCVs marry Filipinos before going back home," he said. "I know the right people at the embassy for this. As standard procedure, we try to talk PCVs ready to get married out of doing so, and we notify parents. But once we're sure they're going to do it, we try to help. We need to talk to your parents. Both of you do. I know you're adults, but please bear with us. Protocol demands we take procedures."

"Can we do that in the next day or two?" Lois asked.

"I'll call them tonight," the director said. "There's a fourteen-hour difference in time zones. We want to be courteous. I'll explain the situation. You are adults. Their permission isn't required, and they can't make you come home. But we need to include them in this."

"We understand," Lois and I concurred.

The hand grenade incident was the center of our conversations with both our parents. Both sets of parents were scared for our safety. Once we got past that, getting married was simpler. Though not easy. But they knew we cared for each other, and we managed without much difficulty to convince them of our feelings and devotion.

"I'm glad you didn't slip and mention the operative

that caused all this," I told Lois back at our hotel room in Malate. "We couldn't prove he was an operative, and it would be denied anyway. The fact that the NPA is belligerent in your area and there's a peace treaty with the MNLF in mine is good enough for now. Let American officials be relieved you're changing your site, and let our getting married make them feel more secure about you. That's a start."

"We need to tell Margaret, Jennifer, and Rhonda," Lois said. "Once the paperwork is done, we'll get them to come to Manila for the wedding."

"Are we going to have a big to-do?" I asked.

"Of course not," Lois replied. "But we want to honor our friends. They made us promise to include them. Our parents are coming. To meet us and each other. It would be nice to have some Peace Corps buddies, too. But the girls are enough."

It took two weeks for everything to be arranged. But it gave our PCV friends and our parents the time to manage their arrivals.

And it gave us time to talk about our future. The one about our life together.

"How are we going to raise our children?" I asked her pointedly. I wasn't as interested in an answer as just talking about the subject I now loved most.

She smiled. I assumed from the thought.

"I had plans on going to California," she began.

"It's open," I replied. "But I have a distaste for California."

"And Mississippi is tasteful for me or something?"

"Okay. Let's see what kind of a lawyer you're going to be. Let's discuss the pros and cons of our soon-to-be environment and the elements in it. Namely you and me."

"So you've already conceded in previous talks that I won't be a housewife. At least seven days a week, full time."

"So." I grinned. "I've already given that away. No negotiation on that matter and no trade-offs. I'm not doing so well. So, I repeat. How are we going to raise our children?"

"To become adults."

"How?" I pushed.

"You're up to something," she said while scoping me out studiously. "What is it? Are you hoping they will be rednecks from the South? Or be Jewish?"

"Bingo."

"Which one?"

"Yes."

"Is there going to be compromise?" she mocked.

"We'll see."

"I bet we do."

I stared at her and waited.

"Which is the most important to you?" she asked.

"You can keep the redneck. I'm not a redneck myself."

"So that's not on the table to compromise either," she said, grinning in victory.

"Should have kept my mouth shut on that one, huh. *Touché*, Ms. Lawyer. You got me on two counts already. Me raising our kids to be rednecks is now a non-starter. So. Are we going to live in California or the South? Or Ohio?"

"What happened to Hawaii?" she chirped. "That's where you were headed this whole time. Now suddenly you haven't even brought it up."

"Hawaii now seems trite to me. Some pipe dream. You're on a roll, my to-be-lawyer, to-be-wife. I've already conceded three points. Struck out already. Am I going to be a househusband before you're finished with me?"

"You tell me. We'll negotiate, but you make your spiel."

"First of all, the South and Mississippi are changing. They're on the way up, and more and more Yankees already think so. I love the Old South, but being Jewish lets me understand I don't love every inch of everything about Dixie. We've got our problems. But it's warmer there in climate and in human interchange. And we've beautiful beaches that can be accessed year round. I love our culture and spirit. Overall. As for problems? Yes, there are certain radical elements among our demography. Let's go home to Mississippi and see if we can enhance some of the betterments in racial harmony and the economy that are occurring there. I don't mean right every wrong. Plus, Mississippi is home to one of us, whereas California isn't for either of us. There aren't enough Jews in Mississippi anyway."

"Aha. Here we go. Slick little maneuver there, Mississippi. First he tugs at my heart strings to love the warmth of the place, meaning weather, culture, history, geography, and people, and then he tugs some more by reminding me that Mississippi is famous for certain social attitudes to which we, hopefully, can contribute a betterment. Then he throws in that there aren't enough Jews. So you're not converting to Christianity, it sounds like, or intending to walk in harmony with the great mystic feminine forces of the universe, either. Am I

179

right? Simple yes or no, even though you're not under oath."

"I like a lot about Christianity," I said. "But you're not attached to Christianity, you already said. And I'm not all that religious. But being a Jew anymore is more like a nationality. I'm not talking about Israel, either, but a Jew's religion is Judaism, and it's a good religion. I love our heritage and all we've grown into through the millennia. I do want to stay Jewish. I'm even attached to our religion. It's ancient but has evolved brilliantly through the ages. It fits modern settings even as it relies on its cultural and religious DNA."

"So back to your original question, then. About how would we raise our kids."

"My take, you mean?"

Her sarcastic expression answered that.

"Jewish," I replied.

"Judaism is so male oriented!"

"All but the orthodox have female rabbis now, and men sit with women in services. The family all sits together."

"What kind of Jew are you? Not orthodox, then?"

"Conservative."

"It's still so male oriented," she complained. "I'm thinking more along the lines of Asherah, which archaeological studies show, by the way, used to have a place in ancient Israel as a consort of Yahweh. Until driven out by later priests and scribes."

"She's pagan."

"She's female," Lois countered. "All the modern religions drove the female goddesses out long ago. Asherah was once worshipped by Jews. I'd be more open to Judaism if the Jews hadn't driven the likes of her out."

"How do you know this stuff? About Jews worshipping Asherah and what happened to that worship."

"I study things. And I want something in my life besides male domination. I'm not against men. Men are good people. The one I chose to spend the rest of my life with, in particular. My problem is that society became so male dominated, beginning thousands of years ago, that the momentum created some pretty unpleasant circumstances I've inherited. Power corrupts, as they say, and a lot of men are damn corrupt. I want to breathe a bit and not look like a radical for it."

"Good points," I acknowledged as I studied her. "To answer about Judaism. Asherah was pagan. That was Elijah's problem with her. He drove out Baal, too. The ancient Hebrews also had, at one time, child sacrifice, at least with some groups. Apparently there was some child sacrifice still going on even at the time of King David in 1000 BC. Even in the Tanakh, or Old Testament, there's all this conflict between strains of paganism and the Hebrew faith. Judaism takes in elements after they've been time tested. God is jealous for a reason. Not to be subject to every whim. We don't stone to death people who violate the Sabbath anymore. Even in the time of Jesus that was happening. People are naturally resistant to change. If we need a heart transplant to save our life, our metabolism still rejects that new heart. For good reason. It might be diseased or dangerous, even if you will die without the new one. So we have to work it out with our immune system, trick it, in order to get a healthy heart in our body to save our own life. So God allows growth, but not whim. The pagan worship of the Canaanites included child sacrifice. Other things too that we now take for granted we don't have. The religion of my ancient tribe, Judah, separated from pagans for a reason. We worked out our covenant with God for a reason. No offense to Asherah, but it wasn't because she was female. It was because she was pagan."

"God is male. I love you, I have no problems with males or maleness. But I don't want to be dominated. Dominant maleness didn't work out."

"God is not male," I countered. "In the original Hebrew word, the one we can't repeat or we profane it, God was not male. God was a verb. Action."

"You're telling me there aren't all these masculine concepts in the Jewish God?"

"There are," I affirmed. "But there are no neuter endings for our nouns in Hebrew. Or in the evolved noun concepts of our God. We have only masculine or feminine. The little skull cap men wear in religious gatherings is feminine. It ends in a-h. It's receptive, like the female, so it's feminine even though worn by a male. Many words to denote God are indeed masculine, but it doesn't mean the Jewish God is male."

I could tell she wasn't convinced.

"Adam, the word for man," I explained further, "was derived from *Adamah* which is feminine and stands for earth. Sort of like 'Mother Earth,' if you want. And from God's interaction with Mother Earth, as stated in Genesis, came man. In the Biblical account, in other words, it took cosmic male and female to create humans."

That explanation seemed to help. She seemed more relaxed now.

"The original name for Eve," I continued, "is *Khavah*. Again, that a-h ending. So, sure, Eve is a woman. Female. But that's not the significance. *Khavah* means life. Life is of feminine origin to the Jew. This tie between the male masculine noun God concept of the ancient Hebrew and the female goddess Asherah that you mentioned, well, the tie was there, but we don't need a pagan goddess for that. We got rid of the pagan, but the female concept is still there. The Hebrew word for God's presence is *Shekinah*. The Shekinah is almost spooky, in a sense, in that the Shekinah was sent to earth to walk among us. And there's the a-h ending again. Meaning Jews see God's presence as female. The word for wisdom is *Hokhmah*. The Hebrew Bible is called the *Torah*, which stands for law. The written law is called *Mishnah*. Almost everything sacred to the Jewish religion is female, in other words. It's as if this covenant between God and His people is a marriage of his maleness to the Jewish feminine sacred. And we were the first to give rights to women and to make sure they were honored and protected. You can find some things that don't seem so, but this masculinization of religions going on back then that you brought up—the ancient Hebrews put a lid on it. They were way ahead of their day. And women are more and more a prominent part of Judaism in modern society. All this to the Jew has ancient roots. It's part of our DNA."

"You're scoring some points, Mississippi, but I'm not really looking for a goddess to worship. Just not a male one, either. So it's nice to see some balance in Judaism. And I understand about Hebrew having masculine and feminine for its nouns. But what I'm really looking for is balance. I don't think the feminine is more important, but I do have trouble with an unbalanced world. My favorite name for deity is 'the Great Mystery,' which is of Native American origin. If everyone used that name, how could people be prejudiced, fight, kill, or discriminate?"

"I appreciate that," I replied. "I feel much the same way about balance. I don't mean exactly like you. You're not Jewish, for one thing. But an appeal in Judaism to me is the great mystery mindset you mention. We're famous for our laws. Over six hundred laws. But most of those deal with Temple rituals. The Temple is over. There has to be some structure in our lives or there is chaos. But without seeking, without innovation, we're these pointy-headed legalists that Christians already think Jews are. Jews have been innovative for millennia. But even in the origins of Judaism each book of the Torah used to be written on a scroll. No vowels, no spaces between words. God's word in the Torah was one word. The priests used to place one end of the scroll against the other to form that one word. No beginning, no end. You couldn't just memorize. You had to seek meaning. There were so many ways you could interpret each passage, as it was presented to us as one word. So that we would search for the meaning. Jews are still searching. Judaism is more about questions than answers."

"I'm not convinced, but I'll convert. I like what I see in you. Maybe this aspect of you really does have something to do with you being a Jew. We'll raise our kids to be Jewish. Don't let this go to your head. I trust you as a person. I just don't want to be dominated in a man's world or by a man's religion. I'm open to becoming a Jew and raising our family in harmony as such. And we'll live in Mississippi, too. You don't owe me except to work things out with me and to worry about my happiness and well being."

"Just like that?" I asked, amazed.

"How do I convert?"

"It takes at least two years. And in the process, the rabbi rejects you at least three times. You have to know you want to be a Jew. Not just because of the religion, but because it's a tough row to hoe. You have to know what you're getting yourself into. You might say part of the covenant with our God is still one of tests. To strengthen us, to sharpen us with questions, and to chasten us. A lot of elements in the world are still aiding God in this, you might say."

"We'll have to wait for when we get married and settled to do it, then," she said. "It gives me time to check it out. But I'm open to the idea."

I almost fell out of my chair. It was as if this was really going to happen. Nothing in my life now but the future. I was ready.

To our delight, an anonymous philanthropist got Lois and myself a room in the Manila Hotel in Malate. It was luxury we had forgotten existed. After such tragedy in Lois' village, this was a welcomed respite. Nothing now to do but get married.

****

"And now," the embassy official said, "with authority granted under the laws that govern the United States and its territories, I now pronounce you man and wife. You may kiss the bride."

Before we kissed, however, we turned to each other face to face as we had planned. We placed our hands on one another's shoulders and looked each other in the eyes. That finished me off. My insides were quivering throughout the whole ceremony as I thought back to our first conversation in San Diego and on to this moment we were sharing now. I barely squeaked out the "I do" when my time came. Now I had a vow to get out, and I didn't have anything left.

I wore the most pathetic, pleading look for mercy as I saw Lois ready to speak our vow in unison with me. The confusion on her face kept it from happening, however. Her expression seemed to ask if I was backing out. I hoped she would figure out we were already married and that I couldn't back out now anyway. My expression begged for help from my struggle. My eyes turned red. *Another clue, Lois, please*, I begged inside.

A look of compassion appeared on her face, and she reached up to stroke my cheek affectionately. The tears exploded after that, and I wanted to crawl away in shame. I rolled my eyes upward, hoping the tears would be trapped. That didn't work, so I turned away to look beyond the chaplain who had married us. I even gagged, trying to breathe a couple of times. Miraculously, I regained my composure, but I still couldn't look at her, knowing the tears and panic would return. I looked beyond her and began to breathe slowly in and out.

Finally, I was ready. I hoped. I looked at her again and saw her smile of pride. She returned her hand to my shoulder and patiently nodded as if asking if I was ready. I nodded back that I was.

She nodded again as if it was a cue. Now. We would say the vow now.

"I will be the one," we said in unison. I could feel the tears returning, but I managed my composure.

Our guests applauded, which embarrassed me even more.

"You may kiss the bride," the chaplain repeated paternally.

And I did. I kissed Lois for the first time as my wife.

"Congratulations," Lois' mother said as she hurried over to hug first her daughter and then her son-in-law, me.

"Congratulations," Lois' father said.

My parents hugged us in welcome.

"Congrats, you two," Margaret, Jennifer, and Rhonda said, smiling at us while they hugged us.

"Congratulations," the embassy and Peace Corps staff said.

Margaret looked Lois in the eye, grinning. "Are you Mrs. Mississippi now?" She snickered wickedly.

"Where should we go for your reception?" Rhonda asked.

"Let's just walk until we find a restaurant that appeals," I replied. "They have a lot of choices in Malate. It's a tourist area."

"It's so appropriate, you two getting married in the Philippines," Jennifer noted.

"You're right, Jenn," Margaret said. "The Philippines got you two married, and it fits that you physically tied the knot here."

"God brought you two together," Rhonda came in. "I never believed in fate until I saw you two."

"That's the truth," Jennifer seconded.

"Isn't it, though?" Margaret said. "Right from the get-go. Right off the bat, in staging in San Diego. Can you believe? Everyone watched these two take to each other and never look back."

The two moms listened shyly but proudly to the story of how their children defined the fate that had filled the last year of their lives in a country they never, until now, had ever thought about before. Finally, the two mothers' eyes met, and they shared their joy together as in-laws for the first time.

"Let's find that restaurant and talk," Margaret suggested. "Instead of standing around in a makeshift wedding room in the U.S. embassy, God forbid."

My mom shook her head as she studied Margaret.

"My word," she said, "y'all have the strongest accents. I never heard anything like it except on TV or something."

"*We've* got accents?" The girls howled. "You sure don't sound Jewish to us."

"How are you going to raise your kids?" Lois' mom asked nervously at the reminder just now of her in-laws being Jewish.

"Let's talk about this somewhere else," Lois suggested, stalling.

"That's right," Margaret stated impatiently. "I've been trying to get us to a restaurant for five minutes now. Come on. This time we're really going to find a place nearby. We have so much to share."

"Let's go," Rhonda insisted. "We're still standing around. We'll talk while we eat. I swear, we're never going to get out of here."

"That's right," Jennifer scolded. "Let's start walking out the door right now. We've got to get the guests of honor on their honeymoon."

"Get real," Margaret howled. "They've been on their honeymoon for the past year."

There was dead silence as everyone looked in embarrassment at the mothers of the newlyweds at this suggestion by Margaret.

"Get us out of here, Margaret," Rhonda said as she pushed her forward.

"I'm so sorry." Margaret apologized. She looked back sheepishly toward the parents, who stood awkwardly silent now. "I've got such a big mouth. Nothing happened, I swear to God. They're still virgins, I swear."

There was a lot to tell our parents. Lois and I rehearsed it on the way as we walked down the block to the first restaurant we found.

"I'm converting to Judaism, Mom and Dad," Lois began solemnly as she sipped at her steaming cup of coffee in the restaurant they found.

"That's lovely, my dear," my mother said cautiously and approvingly while looking at Lois. "But there probably aren't many Jews in the Philippines. I doubt there's a rabbi."

"We're going to Jackson, Mother," I explained. "There's a small congregation, and that's where Lois will start the process of her conversion. We'll wait until then, until after we leave Peace Corps."

"What will you do in Jackson, Lois?" her mother asked in a serious voice. I wondered how much of this Lois' parents could take. They probably felt colonized by now. "I thought you had been accepted at Berkeley Law School."

"I'm going to Ole Miss now, Mother. It's in Oxford, near Jackson. I was going to tell you, but there was so much other going on."

"You're going to Ole Miss, you say?" her mother

asked with a pained expression. "I didn't know the State of Mississippi had a law school. What will you do with a law degree from Ole Miss?"

I looked at my parents to see their reaction to this slander. Their expression was one of sympathy. Lois' parents needed lots of sympathy right now, and I was grateful to my parents for their patience. They could feel insulted another day.

Lois' mother glanced toward her father. "That means our grandchildren will be Jewish, then," she said casually, forcing a smile.

"And Rebels," Lois' dad said with a chuckle. He then looked at his daughter warmly. "We wish you the best, Lois. We know you're doing what's best for you."

"Of course we wish you the best," Lois' mother seconded. "I'm sure you put a lot of thought into all this. There were many things to consider, and you had time to do so. We love you, sweetheart." She looked at me and smiled. "We wish you both the best."

"Thank you," I replied.

Before the conversation was over, Lois and I listened in amazement as Margaret related to our parents how it was she who had stood up to the corrupt officials in their provincial capital in Mindanao, during the epidemic, over the issue of the confiscated powdered milk. Lois chuckled as she praised Margaret's heroics, which added to the story, rubbing my leg appeasingly as she did so.

Chapter 16

Lois and I spent a week with our parents before they went back to America. I hoped my parents, as well as myself, had overcome the stigma of being both Southerners and Jews in the eyes of Lois' parents. But the biggest test was whether my parents could come to grips with having a Yankee as a daughter-in-law. The fact that she chose to become a Jew, and to live in Mississippi, too, helped compensate. It was a week needed for getting to know one another, for sure.

After two days in Manila, we rented a car and drove to Baguio, in the mountains north of Manila and Olongopo. Olongopo was the harbor where Subic Bay Naval Base lay. Almost a mile high, the cool crisp air of Baguio refreshed us all. Lois' parents, in particular, were struggling with the constant smoggy heat in the stale atmosphere of Manila. They saw no wondrous tropical beach, only remnants of Manila Bay. But with the heat so oppressive and the mountain provinces of Luzon so near, we chose the exotic landscape and cool, crisp air over tropical ocean paradise. Even with Baguio near the ocean, we ignored the lowlands completely.

Baguio had an American flavor to it. It was a favorite retreat for the former American colonial officials and was still accessed by U.S. Navy personnel from Subic, embassy staff from Manila, and airmen from nearby Clark Air Force Base. Camp John Hay in

Baguio was run for these Americans.

What I wanted to see, however, were the rice terraces in the adjacent province, where native tribesmen still lived. Modernization had made an imprint on this tribal area, but for the sake of the tourist dollar the locals still dressed in traditional aboriginal-style clothing and lived simply in their small wooden structures. Their clothes were colorful and exposed a lot of skin. The two-thousand-year-old terraces themselves were much advanced over the SALT terraces that the Mt. Carmel missionaries had so far accomplished. From the mountain's top to near its base, huge steps, each five to ten yards wide, were carved into the mountainous terrain and used as rice paddies, or perhaps for vegetables. Some compared it to a wonder of the world.

Depsite how long Lois and I had been away from our home base, we had one more excursion left in us after we said goodbye to our departing parents. To celebrate our official honeymoon. The just-the-two-of-us one. We flew into Davao rather than Cotabato City, for nearby, a ferry ride away across a small inlet, was Paradise Island, a well-named tourist resort that lived up to its billing. There was nothing but coconut trees, brilliant sandy beaches, restaurants, and tourist cabins. It was as if some unwritten law prevailed that kept problems and fast-paced living at bay. There was nothing at all to do but swim in the ocean, bask in the sun, and make love in your cabin. A cabin with electricity and running water.

"I wondered if you would eat *kinnilaw,*" Lois teased me as we sat across the table from each other at what was now our favorite restaurant. "It's raw fish, and that isn't kosher. Right?"

"It's cooked," I answered back with a straight face.

"Kinnilaw is raw tuna or anchovy, love of my life," Lois informed me.

"Yeah, well, raw but cooked. They leave it several hours soaked in vinegar, calamansi, ginger, soy sauce, and I forget what else. Cooked. That's what they say. The acidity of the spices cooks it. Get it?"

"Does your God accept this definition of cooked, sweetheart?"

"To be honest," I said with as straight a face as I could manage, "I'm not sure. I'll ask my rabbi as soon as we get to Mississippi."

Lois picked up a pinch of the delicacy and pushed it playfully into my mouth.

"Somehow I knew it," she said, laughing. "I have the feeling I'm going to have fun being a Jew."

"We Jews, as a species, learned to survive," I replied. "Not just in world history. There's enough problems and rules meshed throughout our cultural DNA. We have to survive ourselves, too, you know."

Our waitress came with the main course. A huge head of a tuna lay on a platter surrounded by massive amounts of white rice.

"Have you ever had this?" I asked Lois.

"Never even knew you could have it," she answered. "I've had fish head vegetable soup in our village. I guess you have to live on the coast to get tuna jaw. That's what I thought you were getting us. Tuna head soup, not just the head of a tuna, big as it is. I thought kinnilaw was the main dish and soup the appetizer. How are we going to eat all this?"

"Somehow," I replied. "I guarantee, you'll die

trying. But it's to die for."

"That's what I'm afraid of, sweets," she said. "There's so much food here."

"The meat inside the jaw of the tuna is so tender. So succulent. And it absorbs the juices as they steam it. It's my favorite Filipino dish. Even more than *adobo*."

"Nothing's better than adobo," she answered.

"Well," I rebuked her, "we'll see what you say after you've had this."

"How are we going to make love after all this food is what I want to know."

"The moon is full," I replied. "We'll walk along the beach holding hands, then sit in a beach chair and look at the light reflection in the ocean. And then nature will figure the rest out by the time we get back to our cabin."

"Can you believe this is the first real beach I've been to since we've been in the Philippines? I've seen Manila Bay. I've seen the port area of Cotabato City. We've always been so short of time we didn't want to waste it going to the beach there. I guess we could have tried."

"Any spare time we had, you always wanted to shop."

"Hey!" She scowled. "My only chances to do so, you know. Anyway, we're here now doing this, and I'm going to pretend it was some cosmic plan. Because this all made a special imprint on me. The first time I saw a glorious tropical beach was Paradise Island, Davao, Philippines, with my husband on my honeymoon. So there."

Those were the magic words. We leaned across the table and kissed. Husband and wife in Paradise.

Just as we sat back again, a waiter walked by pushing a cart with a whole roasted pig. A celebration of some sort was taking place a few tables away. *Lechon*, as Filipinos call it, is the ultimate delicacy. For a rich wedding reception, a barrio fiesta, or a graduation, or perhaps landing a large contract for your corporation.

Lois saw my eyes bug out and immediately tapped me on the head to bring me back down to earth.

"You're a Jew," she yelped. "Down, boy! Get a hold of yourself. We already have more than we can eat, and, no matter how much you wiggle the truth, lechon is still pork. I will write your rabbi myself."

I looked at her with a glazed stare, huffed, then returned to my now blasé tuna jaw.

****

Once back home in Cotabato City, Lois and I got superstitious thinking about it. How the weeks spent together during her school break were a prelude. A warm-up. Spring training for our serious life together.

For now, with our marriage, the regular season began. For the rest of our lives.

I had loved going to visit her before, in her village on the edge of no-man's land. Staying with her in her Nipa Hut. It was a different world. I wanted something different. I got it. I felt like real Peace Corps then.

But suddenly, Lois was with me and life felt tranquil. And with the tranquility it seemed surreal. We went to work together. We shopped together. Went out together. We were an eternal pair. We were really together now. Married. And the Philippines had a charm we appreciated in our married life.

But every day we were reminded of our other

circumstances. The not-as-charming parts. We still had to put up with poverty, overcrowding, a different culture, cockroaches, rats, mosquitos, standing in long lines, poor transportation, and being the center of curiosity everywhere we went. Which was life in a third world country. But the Philippines was our third world country.

The Philippines has a natural beauty, however, in spite of the problems. And we saw that aspect every day. A tropical paradise of beaches, orchids, fruit trees, plush vegetation, and mountains. We didn't feel like Peace Corps Volunteers anymore except for our mission. Which now felt like a job. A low-paying one, but we were young newlyweds. It was fun.

"This is the movie I was telling you about," Lois said. "My mother told me about it when she was in Manila. It's playing here now in Cotabato City. Let's go."

"Have you been to a movie here?" I asked.

"We went in Manila together, silly."

"Yeah, in Makati, their Manhattan," I answered. "I took you there because their movie theaters are comparable to those in America."

"Just what are you saying?" she asked.

"It looks like you're going to experience a new cultural exchange," I said.

"Exchange means I experience something and then offer something cultural back."

I nodded my head. "I meant exchange, just like I said. Your reaction will be the exchange."

She seemed afraid to ask anything else.

The movie was called *The Secret Of The Lost Treasure*. The American title for it was *Romancing The*

Stone. I liked Michael Douglas, but I was in love with Kathleen Turner. After I saw her in *Body Heat* I'd wanted to be vamped like that. But this was a romantic comedy, according to Lois.

"Why is there a stench in here?" Lois asked as we looked for a seat.

"You'll find out."

"What does that mean?"

"You'll find out," I repeated.

"Why are we going to the balcony?"

"To avoid the stench," I replied.

She was ready to say something else, but she resigned herself to finding out on her own.

We had not seen a Tagalog movie since culture training in Zamboanga. Lois knew Tagalog well enough, but there were subtitles in English, as well. We didn't want to go to any more Tagalog movies, though, and language wasn't the problem. Culture was. I liked much of their music. But their movies were melodramatic. I'm using that word because I can't think of a stronger word. Melodramatic on steroids might be more accurate.

Halfway through the movie, two boys in front of us got up and walked to the railing at the edge of the balcony. The light from the movie screen silhouetted the boys as they unzipped their trousers, aimed their body part, and released their excretion into the area below.

"My God," Lois shrieked. She looked at me, disgust mixed with disbelief in her expression. She shook her head, then eased into a humored sneer. "Cultural exchange. I get it now."

This coincided with what proved to be our favorite

line in the movie as Danny DeVito screamed into the telephone at his thug cousin and expressed his displeasure at being stuck in a third world cesspool. That fit perfectly as we watched the boys zip back up and return to their seats. The roaches crawling among the spilled popcorn on the floor barely fazed us after that. The rats at our feet came close to an exchange, however.

Soon we were back in Manila. Since Lois had been reassigned to Cotabato City with me, it was arranged that she was part of the Central Bank group of Peace Corps Volunteers. Now the Central Bank funded us both on our trips to Manila for meetings with the Rural Bank section. Until now, I had stayed in a hostel in a boy's dorm area. This time, at Central Bank expense, we got to share a private room all to ourselves.

We felt like a mom-and-pop store as we rode the buses and jeepneys to my sources of supplies and research. While in Los Banyos to see the scientists and engineers at IRRI, I included a stop at an accounting cooperative, where we shared spreadsheets, database formulas, and programs. They used the Philippine clone desktop, and we exchanged ideas and information on both software and hardware.

There was no denying that we used Manila as a recreational ground during our stay while also accomplishing business objectives. Though the allotment the Central Bank gave us for our time there wasn't much, it and our Peace Corps salary allowed for a few choice restaurants, a night to see Freddie Aguilar sing "Ang Bayan Ko" at the Hobbit House, and, since it was now football season back in the States, enough money left over to spend at an American-owned strip joint that had TVs linked to American sports channels. Even if Ole Miss wasn't playing, I got off to anything resembling Southeast Conference football.

The only Filipinos in the whole bar were the strippers. The rest were Americans. Tourists, servicemen, embassy staff, and businessmen. Lois wasn't sure how much football I had watched in my days here before now, and just how many strip shows I might have enjoyed. She became intrigued, of her own accord, with the life and subculture at this strip joint. She enjoyed studying the atmosphere as much as cheering for my football teams on TV while we sipped on our beers.

"You're working with refugees in Pakistan?" Lois asked a young American man at the table next to us. An American woman his age was attached attentively at his side.

He nodded a yes as he took another sip of his beer.

"This is his last night here," his female companion said, as if answering for him.

"You seem stressed out," Lois said to him.

"He is," the girl answered for him yet again.

"Why's that?" Lois asked.

"Islam," the guy said as he set his beer bottle down in front of him.

I turned my attention to the conversation.

"What about Islam?" I asked with a smile.

"I work with Afghan refugees from the war against the Soviets there," he explained. "There are refugee camps just south of the Khyber Pass. I don't mind the work so much. I was with the Peace Corps here in the Philippines. I worked with refugees in Mindanao a couple of years ago. But at these camps inside Pakistan, a Muslim country, working with Muslim refugees, I'm going bonkers."

"You were in Mindanao in the Peace Corps?" Lois asked.

"We both were," his companion explained.

"So what do you do here?" Lois asked her.

"I got a job, after the Peace Corps, here in Manila with Save The Children. He comes and visits me a couple of times a year now. To try to get his life back, and his sanity."

"Is it so bad, working with Muslims?" Lois asked.

"Not the work," he stated. "But the culture. No alcohol, no scandalizing movies or books. No women. No nothing."

His companion began to stroke his neck in exaggerated displays of concern, as if on cue.

"Lois and I live in Mindanao as Peace Corps Volunteers," I said.

"So where are refugees in Mindanao?" Lois asked them.

"All over the place," the girl answered. "Mostly central Mindanao. At least a half million. Displaced from the civil wars and skirmishes there. And poor people still moving in, looking for a better life, hoping to get something going."

"Central Mindanao. You mean like on the national highway?" Lois asked.

"All along the highway, the marketplaces, the outlying villages. There's nothing for them there. Not for that many. But they had nothing where they came from, either, so Mindanao at least offers a breath of hope. Aid money from the UN and America or Japan comes in for them. They are left alone by the military elite goon squads and the NPA, for the most part. They have enough problems already. They are harmless. They have nothing except hope, false or otherwise. Or maybe to be breeding grounds for propaganda indoctrination, you never know. A lot of the aid money is detoured by the Marcos thugs. Somehow, Marcos and his cronies never have enough. These people have nothing, and Marcos still takes his cut."

The girl kept stroking her comrade's neck with superficial affection, then turned to look at us.

"What do you guys do in Mindanao for the Peace Corps?" she asked curiously.

"We work for a bank," I answered.

Both of them turned toward me to stare.

"A bank?" the girl sneered. "You work for a bank? You came to the Philippines to work for a bank as a Peace Corps Volunteer? To repossess small farmers' farms?"

"We mostly have projects," I replied. I wanted to roll my eyes in sarcasm. I didn't feel like explaining or taking up for myself. "We're computerizing it."

Their stares turned to revulsion.

"Computerizing? You're robots, in other words," the girl said.

She turned away from us and gave even more exaggerated attention to her friend who was ready to return to Pakistan.

This was good, I thought. *I have to remember how he did this*. The guy knew exactly what he was doing. And got everything he wanted from this girl. I felt honored to help on his behalf. Even at the expense of looking like a nerd.

Lois and I returned our attention to SEC football.

Chapter 17

"Marcos called for snap elections for this coming February," Lois said in place of any greeting as I woke up one morning. "It's so sudden," she continued. "Why?"

"America's feeling the heat from backing another despot," I opined. "Reagan doesn't like deserting his friends, but Marcos causes problems. Including the unrest here. It even jeopardizes our military bases here."

"Some in the news this morning say Marcos is doing the snap elections to please Reagan," Lois reinforced. "But not leaving much opportunity for opposition to get anything going. Three months. That's it. The elections will be in February. Except for Cory Aquino, there is no real opposition. She's so popular as a figurehead. Her name alone might defeat him."

"Marcos isn't going to let himself lose," I said. "He'll do whatever it takes, including rig the election. To be honest, I wonder if he could win an honest election."

"What do you mean by that?" Lois asked, incredulous.

"I know he's hated. I believe that. But so many look to him as a paternal figure, almost like royalty. Some are boisterous about him, and the hate for him is very loud, too. But there's this underlying respect for status quo. I think so, anyway. If people just went out and voted today, I wonder what it would be like. But it's going to be interesting. We're watching some kind of history in the making."

"Aquino is popular and represents the future," Lois said. "She's Benigno Aquino's widow. That may be all it takes. We'll see what the three months bring. You might be right. Marcos is counting on you being right. But we'll see how she handles the next three months."

"She's a housewife. He'll make her look a fool." I sighed and kissed Lois on the cheek. "It's history in the making, like I said. Probably nothing will come out of this, but we're here to see. The election will take place two years to the month after we arrived."

Cory Aquino had taken up her husband's mantle following his assassination in late summer of 1983. She was active in demonstrations and protests against Ferdinand Marcos and his ruthless hold on power. A confidant of Benigno Aquino, Salvador Laurel, was the seasoned politician expected to take the forefront against Marcos, but after a million signatures urged her to run, Cory became the candidate instead, with Laurel as her vice-presidential running mate. Soon, another figure entered the scene and was increasingly evident, Cardinal Jaime Sin. It was he who persuaded Laurel to back down and support Cory. With a staunchly Catholic population in the Philippines, Cardinal Sin used his influence, direction, and optimism so that change would take hold.

Marcos followed suit by getting Arturo Tolentino, who was a key opposition figure to him until then, to run as his vice-presidential candidate. Marcos held control of the media and had the machinery and money to get his way. He accused Aquino of being a communist sympathizer and of being inexperienced and naïve. She reminded her countrymen of the dedication of her husband, and of the corruption of the Marcos years.

On election day there was yet another political assassination. In the province of Antique, on the island of Panay in the Visayas, in central Philippines, the governor was gunned down. This added to massive intimidation and fraud at the ballot boxes. Then thirty technicians monitoring the election counts walked out. They claimed that as they monitored the votes, Aquino votes were changed to votes for Marcos.

A week later, Marcos was officially declared the winner of the election. But Aquino ignored the results and declared for a protest march. She also called for a boycott of businesses owned by Marcos' cronies.

Reagan's presidential envoy, Philip Habib, famous for his negotiations for the end of the first Middle East war against the newly founded state of Israel, tried to negotiate a power-sharing arrangement between Aquino and Marcos. Aquino refused it.

"This isn't going away," I said to Lois as we listened to the news.

"Marcos is worried about an uprising in the cities," Lois said. "In particular, Manila. You're the one who explained this to me a year ago. I remember now. You went into such detail with Margaret about it, on one of our visits."

I was having my own flashbacks from all this drama. In 1977 I was working on a *kibbutz* when I heard the news that the president of Egypt, Anwar Sadat, was to arrive in Jerusalem in order to make peace with Israel. Being a Jew, nothing in my lifetime until then had moved me as much as the process that Sadat's arrival in Israel spurred. Peace. There was a chance for real peace in the Middle East.

And now, while I was in the Philippines, on Saturday, February 22, 1986, events spurred an equally deep amount of drama and hope.

Lois and I sat in the living room while my Lola made small talk with us as she chopped food items at the dining table adjacent to us. No one paid the radio any mind. Suddenly, however, Lola was quiet. The quiet felt like a vacuum. I wondered if there was another political assassination announced on the radio.

"The Chief of Staff of the Armed Forces, General Fidel Ramos, and the Defense Minister, Juan Ponce Enrile, have defected from the Marcos government," my Lola explained. Her head kept shaking in bewilderment as she did so.

Though Lois could speak Tagalog fluently, she looked to Lola for explanation.

"General Ramos is even a cousin of Marcos," my Lola said. "This is big news, such big news. There will be a revolution now."

Lois and I looked at each other. This was why we were here, somehow. As part of some destiny. To be a part of the new Philippines. To witness history.

"Cory Aquino," my Lola continued, "is in Cebu now with Carmelite nuns. General Ramos and Defense Minister Enrile have declared their support for her, saying they believe the election was fraudulent and that she was the real winner. They are supporting the reformists in the military. Now we have to find out how many reformists there are, and how many will follow

Ramos and Enrile and join them."

She looked at Lois and me in such a serious way. "May God help us," she said.

"We have to go," Lois declared, staring me in the eyes.

"Go where?" I asked.

"Where my brilliant husband predicted a year ago the revolution would take place. Manila."

"Lois," I said sternly. "This is their revolution. It's for Filipinos. We'll only be in the way. We can't be onlookers. It's not our place. This is not a spectator sport."

"I'm going," she said.

It gave me goose bumps. Not just the revolution taking hold, but this girl I adored that was so a part of my life.

We didn't have the money for plane fare. I had a credit card and charged the amount for both of us. Ramos and Enrile had made their announcement on a Saturday afternoon. Sunday morning Lois and I were on the plane to Manila as hundreds of Filipinos, then thousands, then millions, made their way to the Ministry of Defense complex in the section of Manila called Edsa. A huge human buffer area was created to protect the reformists.

Things moved swiftly. The Catholic Church, already active during the election, renewed their efforts after these major defections. Time was of the essence.

"Cory Aquino called for every Filipino to join her on a march." I related to Lois the things I'd heard from other travelers on the plane as we arrived at the airport in Manila. "She and Cardinal Jaime Sin want to protect the reformists in the military from the army and also to encourage the soldiers to join the reformist movement. It's going on right now. This is why we're here, and it's already happening. We've no time to lose. The military and the masses against them are already forming at Camp Aguinaldo. That's not so far away. We could take a taxi. Things could already be happening."

"And did you hear?" Lois chimed. "This morning when we landed at the airport in Manila I heard some of the other passengers from Cotabato City talking while we waited for our luggage. Last night a plane was highjacked at the Cotobato City airport with some Air Force general on it. When he got here, he was immediately arrested, though, and can't help the rebels after all. Things are really moving fast. What's next?"

I was a Marine during the Vietnam War. That war was so unpopular that much of my generation held protest marches and talked to soldiers to persuade them not to fight, and even confronted armed military and put flowers in the rifle barrels. I had a bitter taste in my mouth about protests because of it. Especially anti-military protests. But as Lois and I stood with the crowd of peaceful revolutionaries in front of Camp Aguinaldo, we watched the millions of Filipinos, led by nuns and priests, holding vigil while doing exactly those things. This eased the anger that was still inside me from years before, during those anti-Vietnam-war days.

Nuns led the masses toward the Philippine Marines and soldiers confronting them at the camp's periphery. To thwart the rifles the revolutionaries faced, the nuns carried rosaries, crucifixes, and Bibles. This was a cause I believed in, the one happening before my very eyes on the streets of Manila.

"Join us," we heard some of the nuns saying to the soldiers. "Who is more important to you, countrymen? Put down your rifles. March with us. We march with Jesus. We march with history. We are the people. We are of you. We are for you."

We could hear strains of singing around us. Quickly it began to pick up. Within minutes, among the throngs, a loud chorus arose. "Onward, Christian Soldiers" we heard. The singing and the spirit moved me to tears. I joined the crowd while holding Lois' hand as we sang with our Filipino brethren. The soldiers refused to fire on their countrymen, instead firing into the air above their heads. Many broke ranks and joined the demonstrators.

It was the climax of spirit, and every ounce was needed. Military tanks stared at us, but the nuns, in particular, held their ground. Inside Camp Aguinaldo, Defense Minister Enrile and Chief of Staff Ramos held press conferences explaining their position to their countrymen and to the world. They knew of their vulnerability and that it might be their fate to die. But they would die taking a stand. They left nothing to fate. They knew the names of unit commanders who were sympathetic to the cause and attempted to coordinate them for when to join the rebellion.

In the crowd, we clustered around anyone with a radio. Knowledge is power, and we needed that knowledge for any feeling of power. We made a stand, but we lived for hope. I carried the spirit of David Ben Gurion, Israel's first prime minister, with me. It was he who had said, "In order to be a realist, you must believe in miracles."

"Enrile and Ramos are moving across the street to

Camp Crame," we were told later that night. "For a last stand. Fighter planes and helicopters are on the way, and Camp Crame is easier to defend."

We were so tired, emotionally as well as physically, but were afraid to leave. Afraid of deserting ship. Of missing history. Lois and I lay down and did our best, on the hard pavement, to take naps, using each other as pillows. Others did likewise. No one could sleep, but no one could stay awake. Catnaps were the best we could do to refurbish our energy.

"Helicopters," some in the crowd cautioned.

"See the jet fighters," a man said, as he pointed toward the sky. "I was in the Air Force. Look, they are not in combat fighting formations. And look at the men in the helicopters. They have their forefingers and thumbs forming an L-shape. That stands for Laban, Cory's party. These aircraft are joining us. They are not here to destroy us. They are here *for* us."

Many around us cheered.

Enthusiasm spread through the crowd. Not only were the aircraft not firing, they showed signs of joining the rebels, as the man with us had explained earlier. Then, like a line of standing dominoes, a chain reaction occurred. The last traces of loyalty to the dictator fell. The rebels swarmed the Presidential Palace, and all mass media fell into rebel hands.

The next day Marcos departed.

"I was one of three people in the Central Bank," my friend of a high position told Lois and me a few days later, "who knew the codes to the vault where all the gold was stored. This gold was of our national treasury, but in the dictatorship, it meant it was the personal treasure of Marcos. You must tell no one this, what I am going to tell you. You are American, and I can tell no one here. I feel obliged to leave an account of things I have witnessed. You cannot use my name nor repeat where you got this information. But my conscience demands I tell someone, and you are the ones," he said, looking at Lois and me, "that I trust the most of all the Americans I know. And you are in the Peace Corps. If I told an American official, word would get out."

My stomach was getting queasy listening to my friend. I felt the most special person alive. I had known he was high up in the bank, but with no idea he had so much power.

My Central Bank friend continued, "I was ordered to give the vault's code to the Marcos regime, so they could take all that gold away with them. I was informed, but I don't know if it is true, that American special forces drugged President Marcos and flew him out of the Philippines to Guam and on to Hawaii. People in his regime took out the gold. Actually, not all of it, but a great amount, for him to live in exile. It was supposedly a small price to pay to free the Philippines of him. Even the Americans didn't want to deal with him anymore, and now that it had come to a head, they wanted him out. I'm telling you this because, to be honest, I feel expendable. Something might happen to me. I need someone to know, my friends. Just in case. Even if you told someone, people would not believe you. But that's why I'm telling you. Just for someone to know. Not for you to do anything. But just for you to know this. No one would dream I would tell a Peace Corps Volunteer. You are safe."

I nodded that I understood. I was dumbfounded but

felt honored. I was needed. In my own insignificant way.

When Marcos reached Hawaii, he claimed he had no idea he was being ousted. It was heroic, in a sense, that he did not order the troops to attack the crowds of protestors in the demonstrations. The order was out, but Cardinal Sin had intervened. President Marcos, knowing he had few options left, wanted to talk to the Cardinal, almost as a confessor. Cardinal Sin, so we were told, advised him of his legacy. How history would portray him as the one who shot down the nuns and the masses, just to hold on to power. Marcos told the troops not to shoot. Shortly after that, he was gone.

The streets were jubilant as the Philippines swore in a housewife as their next President. Everywhere, ribbons of yellow waved around the country. The American song, "Tie a Yellow Ribbon Round the Old Oak Tree" spurred this significance.

With the radio and TV stations now able to broadcast freely again, it wasn't Cory Aquino who appeared first. Nor was it Cardinal Sin, or General Ramos, or Minister Enrile. Filipinos turned to music for their inspiration. Freddie Aguilar was the first to appear on free television, where he sang, for all to hear, "Ang Bayan Ko." My mind raced to my first night there. And I was still there. I had witnessed it all. Every bit of it. As a Peace Corps Volunteer in the rice paddies and barangays. And in the streets.

Chapter 18

There's fulfillment in a relationship. Being with Lois all these years, I've been keenly aware of being a man, and of my role as such. I feel a satisfaction in my relationship with her and in being father to our children. And I feel appreciation for being with a woman as in being part of a whole. As if part of some divine plan. A beautiful plan with direction on a path that seems ordained. I feel at one with Lois and at peace with myself and my life because of it.

They call the Peace Corps the toughest job you'll ever love. That hits the nail on the head as far as I'm concerned. I can't think of anything I'm more proud of than my years in it. I did so much complaining and surviving then, in the Philippines of those days, that I didn't have time to consider how much I loved what I was doing. I think about it a lot now.

I doubt we accomplished one tenth of what we set out to do in the Peace Corps. But I know I'm better off for having done all I did, and I bet the people I met are, too. There is happiness in my memories.

Lois and I often remind each other of that happiness. It's where we met. It's where we fell in love. It's the honeymoon we had before we got married.

To my surprise as much as hers, Lois loves it in Vicksburg. She takes Interstate 20 over the bridge and across the bend of the mighty Mississippi River on her

212

way to and from work in Louisiana as a real estate lawyer. She claims she has no regrets for turning down law school at Berkeley to marry me. She got her law degree from my alma mater, and we're all rebels here in Vicksburg together.

At every opportunity, we share the vow we made at our wedding ceremony. It takes us back to its significance in Mindanao, and our experiences there. *I will be the one*. A statement of survival not just of the fittest person, but of the fittest protecting others and the species. King Arthur had his Camelot. Third World or not, we had our Mindanao, and it left us bonded with the Filipinos and with each other for life.

A few words from the author...

Born in Harlingen, Texas, on October 7, 1948, where I grew up and worked on a cotton farm, I graduated from Harlingen High School in 1966. I attended Texas A&M beginning in Summer 1966. In January 1970 I dropped out to enlist in the United States Marine Corps, where I served as an enlisted man, attaining the rank of Sergeant, with an honorable discharge after three years. I worked as a computer programmer afterwards in Houston and as a civil servant for a US Air Force Base in Frankfurt, Germany. I traveled and worked in Europe for two years, which included flying to Israel in October 1973 to aid the Jewish State in the Yom Kippur War. I was also in Greece in the summer of 1974 when the war between Greece and Turkey erupted over Cyprus. I was stuck on the Greek Island of Ios for part of that war, until I managed to catch a boat to Athens just in time to watch the Greek military dictatorship fold. I returned to Texas A&M in the Fall of 1976 to finish my Bachelor's degree in Business Management and returned to Europe afterwards, and then also to Israel, where I lived for almost a year. I later taught English in Taiwan before returning home to get a Master's degree in Agricultural Economics in 1980, which I received in 1982. I joined the US Peace Corps in 1984 and served for three years in the Philippines. In 1987 I began work for the Swiss government as a computer programmer until 1998. I have worked in the IT department of Texas A&M since 1998. I have three children, am presently divorced, and am Jewish.

CPSIA information can be obtained
at www.ICGtesting.com
Printed in the USA
LVHW080811310522
720098LV00015B/737